The leading ruptor dissolved in smoke and exploded flesh. The second ruptor screamed in through the debris, its body passing scant inches above the canopy. Its stinger reached the mark and Sergeant Goudsmit slumped over, dead. The flier, left pilotless, nosed down, scraped through the geron bushes for two hundred yards, falling to pieces all the way. . . .

Wade and Martin scrambled out of the wreckage and immediately took cover. They were just in time, as the ruptors began to zero in on them. Ruptor after ruptor hurled itself down on them. Dirt gouted into the poisonous air as sting after sting scraped along the ground seeking to impale the humans crouching beneath the scrap of cover. Then, suddenly, there was silence.

"What are the ruptors waiting for? Perhaps they don't like nighttime. Maybe they've gone."

"No. They'll be back. . . ."

ON THE SYMB-SOCKET CIRCUIT

BY
KENNETH BULMER

ace books

A Division of Charter Communications Inc.
A GROSSET & DUNLAP COMPANY
1120 Avenue of the Americas
New York, New York 10036

Also by Kenneth Bulmer:

THE HUNTERS OF JUNDAGAI

I

THREE OR FOUR TIMES in the last six days his alice had squirted him up the funny muscle and Matthew Wade had welcomed the light relief at this point of his self-imposed exile.

This computer, now. . . Men needed computers so much that playing jokes on them had become on addict's vice.

He had to remember that if his impersonation of an ordinary human being could continue with any degree of success he must consistently maintain a mature responsibility to the antics around him. The sober knowledge battled freakishly with obsessive desires to abandon all responsibility. This administration computer of Star House, now, from which he expected merely to extract routine personnel information, acted on him like a highly volatile drug.

"Hey, Wade, are you nearly through?" Eva Vetri called across the computer room. Her slim brown fingers fondled the fur of her alice and a shaggy sheaf of papers and tapes ruffled around her as she gestured violently. "I've a mess of details to get out about the harvest—"

Wade ignored her. He pressed his hands flat on the warm plastic-metal of the computer fascia. How supremely giggle worthy it would be to punch into the computer a nursery rhyme. Say one of those trapezoidal language fabrications from Giorgione's Planet, or a simple mnemonic that would echo and reverberate within the electronic pathways of this insensate machine's mechanical mind. Great fun!

Or—and how sneakily diabolical that would be —just for a moment turn on those circuits in his own brain he had switched off when he'd left Altimus and reach into the computer and pump the hysteresis cycles of "The little Preet had a treet whose freetless greetings calokreeted it," directly into the scientific marvels of the computer's innards.

Gosh, wow, boy oh boy!

"Wade. Are you all right?"

"Perfectly, thank you, Miss Vetri." He spoke with a difficulty he concealed with habitual professionalism. An ordinary human being would react with predicted patterns in given situations, he knew that well enough. It was just that, right now, he wanted to turn on and have a giggle ball.

"You look—you're sure you've got the hang of that GBM?" Her small brown face showed concern, a wrinkling between the eyebrows, a softer pouting of the full lips. The annoyed fluttering of the papers stilled although her hand continued its sensuous stroking along the fur of her alice. "That's the most complex computer this side of Sjellenbrod, and it costs—"

"It costs more than our combined salaries per minute," he said more firmly, with a patched smile. "I'll be all through in just a moment."

What had he been about? If he switched on those extra circuits in his brain the coords of Altimus would know, *would know* . . . the rank fear of Altimus stank in his mind.

Forcing himself, but without hesitation, he rapped out the routine inquiry and then stood up, indicated the vacant chair.

"It's all yours, Miss Vetri."

She sat down and twitched her alice into a more comfortable position over her shoulders, poising her hands above the input. As a human being she presented certain ticklish problems for Matthew Wade.

"There's been a lot of—well, you know, funny sort of sickness about. If you're feeling peculiar—"

"I'm quite all right, thank you, Miss Vetri. I appreciate your concern."

"—have Doc Hedges check you out."

"Thank you."

"Kolok Trujillo's due in this afternoon. He's a big man in the galaxy. I hear he always brings about a hundred hangers-on wherever he goes. There'll be a ball tonight."

"Yes."

He picked up his printout, that chattered through its slot like Moloch spitting out bones, and walked off.

"Hey, Wade!"

He turned. Eva Vetri looked up with a brown sparrow motion of her sleek head.

"Didn't you have any files?"

"Ah, no."

She frowned. Her own information papers billowed on the rest, bulging beneath the clip.

"Don't tell me you keep your data and your code in your head?"

"It was only a tiny routine matter," he said and continued walking, thankful for his alice, which at

7

that moment hiccuped and gave him breakaway cover.

"Thanks, Sinbad," he symbed, and the response formed a pattern of amused pleasure in his mind. On arrival on Ashramdrego, when he had been fitted with his life support system, he'd been disappointed and obscurely alarmed at the lack of telepathic quality on the part of the organism on which his existence depended. On Catspaw he'd achieved a friendly relationship with Boris in half a day. But here even in six days he'd come to see a counter benefit. He'd never developed as close a relationship with Lon Chaney, his camouflage cloak, as had many other people with theirs and, aware of his need for isolation and aloofness, had felt no loss. Lon Chaney hung now supinely down his back. That very ego-succoring apartness he must cultivate benefited by the puzzling muffling of symb contact with the alices here on Ashramdrego.

He left the computer section of Star House—like most of the structures here simply fashioned from local materials—and headed for the corner block housing personnel, across from a flier park with the CT Building partially hidden beyond. The sun Ashram shone down beneficently. From space the sun blazed red and golden, but here on the surface of Drego, the third planet, the poisonous atmosphere turned those fiery colors to burning blues and verdigris greens. Long sinuous wafts of toxic gases lay like afternoon cloud shadows over the nearby hills and the muted brilliance of topaz and sapphire and amethyst drowned the planetary surface in a ghostly dry land image of undersea.

He breathed in deeply, letting his lungs creak and

savoring the out-of-doors feeling. Sinbad burped amicably.

On a planet like this he could well understand why some people opted out of the symb-socket circuit and became permanents, like the personnel of Kriseman, who lived here all the year around.

Just what had possessed him—the word was in noway too strong—back there before the computer he had no idea, apart from a frightening feeling of irresponsibility, of juvenile light-headedness, of an adolescent atavistic fecklessness, he could analyze no further. He had been taught that most humans, ordinary humans, were still children at heart and he supposed, not without a tremor of distaste, that his recent intimate contact with them had begun to work insidiously on him.

Between the complex of office buildings and housing enclaves of the Kriseman Corporation Headquarters flowering Dregoan shrubs grew in painted profusion and flower beds bloomed in autumnal splendor. Semisentient gardeners tended the plots. People strolled along the flagged paths. As though mindful of his duty, Matthew Wade avoided them without conscious effort. A few yards ahead he saw the tall and portly form of Silas Sternmire, the planetary director, the big man himself, and he made to avoid him, too.

A heavy, prestigious man, whose features reflected the self-opinionated, self-gratifying, self-importance of one responsible for a whole planet's well-being and overly conscious of that scarcely demanding chore, was how Sternmire had been summed up by Wade at their first interview. Completely without humor, with two deep parallel indentations at the corners of his mouth, he could have reacted to the names T. S. Eliot and W. H. Auden as though confronted by open cesspools.

The planetary director espied Wade. A bright, chuckling expression fleeted across those doughy features. The unyielding man bent like a camel going down on its knees.

"Walsh, isn't it?" Then in a quick, bubbling voice: "Hey, Walshy, I bet I c'n beat ya at marbles. C'mon."

The portly figure knelt, trousers straining. Sternmire's thick fingers flicked. Glass spun flickeringly in the sunlight.

Unbelieving and yet forced to believe by what he saw, Wade realized the big man did want to play marbles. The speech patterns and values bewildered Wade.

Still unsure of normalcy in this unfamiliar world, still strange even after Tiberious and Catspaw and Takkarnia, still uncertain just how adults were expected to behave, he knelt beside Sternmire.

"Where's yer alleys, Walshy? Say—I'll lend ya some of mine. Here, I c'n lick you easy!"

Sternmire's life support system rippled furrily along his shoulders and back. Ignoring his alice, Sternmire, whose flushed and happy face reflected all the joys of boyhood, spun and flashed his marbles in the dust of the walk.

The feel of the marbles between Wade's fingers unleashed a gush of memories.

The past-destroying violence of those memories washed up a maelstrom of bric-a-brac: hot happy afternoons playing with the other kids on the back lot; wondering about Dagda; diving and swimming mother naked in the water-scooped pool below the spillway; scrumping for golden apples where every breaking branch signaled a helter-skelter rout; reading under the bedclothes late into the night; a score of boyish memories flickered through his operating brain like goldfish past an aquarium light.

Then, like the last bright frame of a film rustling through the projector, those old happy memories vanished to be replaced by the abrupt vision of his parents' faces, serious, worried and unsure about his future, looking at him already as ordinary people looked at coords. He did not have to recall his life after that, when the calm-faced man in the blue cloak and silver girdle had taken him to Altimus, for that life was so intimately a part of himself, so essentially what he was now, what he was trying to deny, that only by this apparently stupid fight and return to the galaxy could he hope to regain the boy he once had been.

"C'mon, Walshy, it's your go."

"All right, Mr. Sternmire—"

"Hey! You tryin' to be funny or sump'n? My old man's not around. I'm Gus. You oughtta know that, stupe!"

"Yeah, sure, Gus," Wade said, trying to catch the boyish intonations. "I'll match you, and I'll lick you, sure."

"Nah! Not me. I'm the best. Just lookit that!"

Sternmire's thick fingers flicked with remnants of vanished skill. Glass sparkled against the dust.

"Not bad," said Wade. Carefully, betrayingly more at ease with relationships on this juvenile level, he flicked his own marble. Glass spat and glittered.

"Hoo, boy!" chortled the director, his thick face creased and sweating, the ruff of hair bedraggled

11

like a drunken cockatoo's. "Not bad. But I'll beat-ya!"

The planetary director pushed at his alice, his thick fingers groping around the symb-socket at the base of his neck where the life support system's blood circulation was joined to his own. He didn't notice what he was doing. All his concentration was bent on flicking his glass alley, on beating Wade.

Sternmire's alice didn't like those sausagy fingers probing at him. He rippled chestnut fur tinted green by the hollow light, unwrapped a beady black eye. The director completely engrossed in his game of marbles scratched the skin around his symb-socket, fumbled in toward that spot where the two circulatory systems twined. His alice burped.

"You should be more careful, Mr. Stern—uh, Gus."

"Wazzat, Walshy? Nittering itch. . . . C'mon! It's all on your pitch!"

The glass alley smooth in his fingers, Wade cast a worried glance at Sternmire's fingers scratch, scratch, scratching at the alice's arterial probe.

"C'mon, Walshy! You chicken!"

If this was truly how ordinary humans behaved. . . .

"Go easy!" Wade had to say, snapping the words out through his own feelings of frustration. On Catspaw there had been nothing like this. To have to live among continuing adolescents—and because of his own choice! "Careful of your alice."

"Wazzat?"

A Mephistophelian brand of fury caught at Wade in the frustrations his agonized decision to reject his calling as a coord had brought. In renouncing his special birthright he had renounced his own justification for exercising those rights; he had outlawed himself.

"Leave your alice alone, Gus, for Astir's sake!"

"Alice? What you talking about? Alice's gone riding on her fancy new pony. You know that, Walshy. C'mon, let's get with it!"

Thick fingers poking, probing. . . . Marbles splashing sparks of brilliant color in the Ashram sunshine. . . . The gently zephyr breeze of poison gas Dregoan atmosphere. . . .

Sternmire's alice hiccuped. He wriggled and then extended three of his slender, jointed legs, their toe-claws varnished a brilliant carmine. The movement on the director's neck and shoulders upset him. He gave a vigorous, youthful push, carelessly shrugging.

"Goddamned itch! Are you gonna play or not, Walshy?"

"This has gone far enough—" began Wade.

Sternmire suddenly spun around. He jumped up convulsively. He clapped both hands to his neck, the broad palms crushing down on the alice as though to hold it there. Seeping redness oozed around his symb-socket.

"No!" Sternmire screamed. He lost his boyish glee. His hair flapped. His pudgy face showed scored lines of absolute horror. "Help! Help!"

A shadow moved across Wade. A voice, terse, harsh, angry, crisped orders.

"It's the director! His alice is going! Get a lung here—*fast!*"

A face bent momentarily toward Wade and he recognized Luis Perceau, the Kriseman Corporation's defense officer on Ashramdrego. Perceau, a bulky, blocky, cropped-haired dynamo of bone and muscle, hoisted Sternmire like a hop pocket.

"Wade, isn't it? I'll remember *you!*"

Activity boiled between the flower beds. A white-coated medic charged through a carefully tended plot of Dregoan roses sending petals flying in a confetti of panic. Clerks and chem lab techs clustered. Voices rose high, shocked, excited.

Wade stood back. Danger groped for him here.

In his hands he still held three of the glass alleys. All the confusion displeased him. Glass crushed together in his fingers. His impersonation must have broken down.

The medic's white coat, cut and flared where his alice snugged on his shoulder, blotted out Wade's view of Sternmire. The planetary director continued to yell. Perceau, his cropped hair glistening like a wheat field after the reapers, grabbed for the lung.

"Snap it up!" shouted Perceau.

Between them they held the director long enough to enable the medic's job to be done by Perceau. The medic flipped the hose tap. The three gyrating men twisted around. Wade saw Perceau slap the plastic face mask over Sternmire's ghastly face. Now Sternmire breathed standard nitrogen/oxygen air. They strapped the air cylinder to his back. It hung there, alone, a mechanical replacement for the alice's oxygenating function, good for sixty minutes of life.

Sternmire's face through the glazed blueness shrank to a pinkish facsimile of health. Wade realized he had been holding his own breath all the time. He let it out now ond expelled the poison gases of Ashramdrego that Sinbad rendered him capable of breathing.

14

Luis Perceau swung heavily toward him.

"You! Wade! I'll see you—"

Perceau stopped in mid-harangue. He saw the marbles powdered in Wade's hands, diamond-dusting to the walk.

He reacted.

"Here's another!"

He dived for Wade, grabbed his hands, spun him, twisted his arms up behind his back, pressed his hands away from his alice.

"Don't touch your alice, you fool!"

"But I'm—" began Wade.

Lon Chaney, his camouflage cloak from Samia, wriggled his sixteen legs and swirled out of the way. Wade's abrupt bitter memory of the degrading fist fight on Takkarnia erupted in his mind; he had solemnly promised never to remember Takkarnia again.

"You want another lung?" yelled the medic. He started around Sternmire, who leaned in, grasping the medic's arm, unwilling to allow a savior to depart.

"Not yet. The alice looks in good shape, but you never can tell. With this goddamned juvenile sickness striking everywhere, you just can't be sure." He snapped the last order as though on parade. "Keep that lung on ready alert, medic!"

"Yes, sir!"

Sternmire, propelled by the medic, followed by Wade in Perceau's custody, they marched along the walk. Clerks and techs fell back, and whispers and shocked comments expressed eloquently the suppressed fear of contagion that gripped these people in face of a sickness their medical experts had been unable to combat.

Wade realized that Luis Perceau, for all his pseudo-martial pomp and bearing, must be a very brave man. The medic, too.

The olive drab tunic, cut to accept the alice, with the bronze buttons and the pair of dummy plastic hand grenades, of a pattern obsolete for a thousand years, attached over the breast pockets, the bits of gilded brass, the gilt leaf edging to his cap, these status symbols made of Perceau a laughingstock in the eyes of Wade. And yet . . .

"I'm perfectly all right, thank you." Wade spoke with stiff formality. "The Director wished to play me a game of marbles and I felt it incumbent on me to do so."

"A right pair of nutters," remarked the medic. His face, a raw beefsteak with three o'clock shadow, betrayed contempt and pity. Here strode a man clearly of the symb-socket circuit. Of fear, wherever he kept it, none showed on that pugnacious face.

Ahead, along a sidewalk between the personnel building where Wade's office was located and the flier park, the abruptly stark outline of the CT Building showed. Built of white concrete, windowless, possessing a single door giving access to the massive airlock, the Condition Terran Building stuck out in the softer Dregoan architecture like a motor torpedo boat among a flotilla of yachts.

"You'll be all right once we get you inside," rumbled Perceau reassuringly. "And there hasn't been time for this Astir-forsaken atmosphere to eat at the director's eyes and skin." He took a fresh hitch on

Wade's wrists, run up his back. Wade winced.

"It's really not necessary—"

"You'll be just fine. Don't worry."

Resignedly, Wade symbed Sinbad: "Sorry about this."

The response pattern formed with a line of puzzlement riding through the amusement. A sensation of pleasure at glass spheres, winking and bouncing in the sunlight, of disappointment at a game unfinished. . . . But amusement, the old giggle muscles in full play, remained, as usual, the dominant response pattern from Sinbad.

"You're just like a kid yourself," symbed Wade with affectionate tolerance.

News had already reached ahead of them and as soon as they marched through the inner valve the ordered efficiency of the Planetary Terminal caught them up in its separate and articulate world. Here, and as far as Wade knew only here, on the surface of the alien planet Drego could be found conditions in which an Earthman could live as he might back home on Earth. A direct and hermetically sealed tunnel led from the CT Building to the spaceport. Bypassing that the little procession headed directly for the symbiosis theater.

"Bring the director straight through to number three," said Doctor Marian Anstee. "We're going in to wash up straight away. I just hope the psychophysiological shock hasn't done too much damage." She saw Perceau lugging Wade. "Not so urgent?"

Perceau grunted and heaved up on Wade's arms as though he had attempted to evade custody.

"He hasn't touched his alice, doctor. I've seen to that."

17

"Good." Doctor Anstee spared no further regard for Wade. She took off for the theater at a run, her slim legs flashing, her fair hair disarranged, her face with its large eyes and soft mouth purposeful. Her own alice lay curled up and quiescent on her shoulder, exposed beyond the edge of the white gown she began to shed as she ran. The alice's legs were tucked in and holding and his eyes were fast closed. Here, in an atmosphere which the alice could breathe comfortably and not have to carry the respiration of his symbiont, he tended to doze off.

Sternmire's weak gestures quieted as an eepee trolley took him from the medic. Wade saw the director strapped down on the pallet by the electroplasm's extensible feelers and whisked away toward the theater. Somewhere a siren that had been hooting since their arrival stopped.

In the person of Sternmire and his need for a new alice, mankind was once more unmistakably exerting the right to stay alive on the alien planets of the galaxy.

II

"Look, Perceau. I'm perfectly all right. Really I am."

"Yeah? So how come you're playing marbles with the director?" Perceau snorted. "Marbles. I reckon you've both lost yours." He snorted again, pleased. Wade gestured helplessly. "I thought I was doing the right thing."

"Right thing!" Perceau's brief moment of humor

vanished. His heavy jaw dropped. "With the director goading his alice like a half-witted kid poking a snake?"

"I warned him. I tried to stop him."

"There's no time to warn a guy monkeying with his alice on the symb-socket circuit. You know that. You've got to grab him quick and shove a lung over his face fast."

"Yes."

"The poison gases down here may be only trace fractions, but they'll kill you stone dead—and with a green face and bulging, suppurating eyeballs and spitting your guts all over the scenery, too."

"I know."

"You'd better have Doc Hedges check you over. You sure you're not feeling funny?"

"Far from it—on one level."

"What does that mean?"

Wade shook his head. "Nothing. I'll go see the doctor."

"We've got Kolok Trujillo coming in this afternoon—one of the biggest corporation directors in the whole goddam galaxy after his supply of gerontidril —and this has to happen."

The importance of directors of corporations dealing throughout that part of the galaxy so far opened up by Homo sapiens was not to be denied. Clearly Defense Officer Luis Perceau had much on his mind.

"Those Godforsaken ruptors have been stripping the bushes over in Beta Five plantation all week, and Tom Martin's away doing what he can. How I'm supposed to keep them under control with the equipment and personnel I'm allocated I don't know." Perceau's ugly jaw stiffened. "I'd like to carry out a planetwide extermination policy! Not just this continent. That's the only way to deal with that kind of vermin."

Matthew Wade had heard of the ruptors but so far had not seen any live specimens. Pinned and framed behind glass in the administration building's lobby a set of three had been mounted, no doubt, Wade had thought when he'd first halted, arrested by their brilliant blue and brown menace dead behind glass, to keep before the personnel the vivid image of this animal form that threatened the profits of the Kriseman Corporation.

His first impression had been that here were gigantic chordate bees: huge bristly bodies with spatulate wings spread in a gossamer of power, short and chunky heads with faceted eyes and machined jaws, underslung stingers that projected from their tails and raked forward of their bodies to extend a good three feet in advance of their heads. They looked like enormous winged prawns curled for action, like nightmarish winged tarantulas with stings unlimbered beneath instead of above.

At their tips those stingers bifurcated into pincers, scissorlike razors of clipping destruction that could bite down a carefully planted row of geron bushes and surgically prune a wide swathe of leaves. To watch a ruptor in action, so Wade had been told in disgust, was like seeing an insane eepee hedge pruner hewing its way through the center of a line of bushes and discarding leaves in a shredding of outflung fronds.

"A dusting of hormone powder all over—that'd stop 'em dead in their tracks, by Astir!"

"A bit drastic though, Mr. Perceau. I mean," Wade smiled. "I thought they were fliers."

Perceau's glare in return lacked nothing from his armory of dogged contempt. "You a nut, or something? You'd better cut along to Doc Hedges. Me, I'm for the Split Infinitive. And remember, Wade, I've got my eye on you."

"I feel flattered."

And Matthew Wade walked off, not entirely satisfied with his exchange with the defense officer but obscurely elated.

Through the airlock and outside the CT Building Sinbad gave a few experimental belches and then settled down to his regular rhythm of breathing. Wade's alice was providing the means of life not only to Wade himself but also to Lon Chaney, and the alice seemed to thrive on the extra load.

Striding out between flower beds onto the main walk again Wade paused a moment. No sign of the recent emergency remained except a colored scattering of Dregoan rose petals being swept up by an eepee gardener. The semisentient gardener, electronically structured and isotope powered with a scrap of protoplasmic matter to provide a degree of virtuosity to its micro-miniaturized computer brain, could perform a surprising number of tasks. In less need of costly detailed programming than a true robot an electroplasm provided relatively cheap and efficient servant units to humanity.

The people moving about the walks and passing from office to office of the Kriseman Corporation Headquarters complex gave no heed to the electroplasm. Eepees to them were merely life artifacts to be used as seemed proper.

21

Wade gazed across to the purpled hills where level strands of emerald and amethyst gases hung like tobacco smoke in an overheated room. Between these nearer hills and the headquarters, as beyond them way past the Fractured Hills, stretched the unending rows of geron bushes. Each bush received unremitting care and devoted attention. Every plantation so far cultivated in the constant expansion across this northern continent of Ashramdrego was numbered and counted and computerized into the equations that represented life, power and profits.

He skirted the railed enclosures where animated bamboos whistled and lashed the air in frenzy seeking to seize the spinning, dancing motes of insects feeding on the flower heads; blind beggars striking at ragamuffins.

Already he had promised himself he must inquire more deeply into the motivations of men in the galaxy on this empirical level; all the learned knowledge of Altimus had remained almost entirely on the theoretical level. One deeply rooted reason for his coming to Ashramdrgo had been the desire to slow down. He fancied he'd joined the symb-socket circuit originally without realizing the impossibility of slowing down in the galaxy, using the more obvious reason, the more practical reason, that Altimus didn't take much interest in the symb-socket circuit.

Perhaps, the notion occurred to him with a suspicious little frolic up his giggle muscles from Sinbad, just perhaps he could open up a little in this end of the galaxy; relax, let life flow, act with the bonhomie natural to him.

He went across to the hospital, its white-painted walls reflecting a chiaroscuro effect from the declining sun, the wafts of tinted gases and the mirror pools decorating the lawns. Small but well equipped, the hospital had been forced into coping with more work here since the Kriseman Corporation had opened up the planet after taking the concession against stiffer opposition than had been expected. Going inside, he felt pleasure that Sinbad, in automatically adjusting the atmosphere to his terrestrial needs, filtered out all the normally disturbing smells prowling in even the most delicately run of hospitals.

The eepee at reception flashed some colored lights, clanked a cog or two and then droned: "Doctor Hedges is not available at this time."

About to let rip a choice backwoods cuss word, Wade chopped it off and, instead, said: "Hi, sister."

He trusted he had produced the greeting well.

Sister Olive Cameron pushed her white uniform cap up, its starch shining, and half-smiled at him.

"What Archibald says is correct, Mr. Wade. Doctor Hedges isn't available. He's—"

"Oh, I can guess." Wade smiled at Olive Cameron. He found her profession a way in to a more easy relationship with her than with Eva Vetri. Her figure, with its solidly dumpy proportions and bountiful endowment of breast and thigh, moved with a bouncing grace. Her alice, a species lighter than general and with a golden chestnut fur, rippled sensually as she stroked it with her left hand. Her face, smooth, full lipped, blue eyes, betrayed a tension of feeling he did not feel at liberty to probe.

"I can guess," he repeated. "Just where I've come from."

"The CT Building. What with this accident with the director and Doctor Marian Anstee being tied up, Doctor Overbeck requested assistance from Doctor Hedges in dealing with the Kolok Trujillo party." She sniffed. "Although Doctor Overbeck asking for assistance from anyone surprises me."

"Ah, Doctor ·Hedges is a medical doctor, though, isn't he?"

"Of course." This woman's professional devotion to her doctor although expected was sincere. "And he's not altogether happy with the whole conception of 'doctors of symbiosis,' I can tell you—although perhaps I shouldn't—"

"That's all right, sister. Even with the symb-socket circuit in full swing, after all these years since Doctor Arliss completed his work, symbiosis is still under attack. But we wouldn't get far on Ashramdrego without it, would we?"

Olive Cameron stroked her alice, which yawned in a wide gaping of his long sucking tube. She did not reply directly.

"And, Sinbad," symbed Wade, "you just remember how I'm sticking up for you."

The response pattern jiggled with amusement and a little prod of delight at relished powers.

"You are all right, Mr. Wade? Why did you wish to see—"

"I was with the director when he—when he—he asked me to play marbles, so—"

"You didn't!"

"I did."

She put a hand to her mouth, smiling.

"I'd have loved to have seen that."

"Luis Perceau saw it. He told me to see the doc."

He turned to go, smiling. She put out a hand and touched him on the bare forearm.

"Oh, Matthew. There's to be a ball tonight. There always is when a big party like the Trujillo one comes planetside. We're far enough away from Earth, heaven knows. The orgy should be fun, too. You'll be there?"

Her eyes did not focus on him and a flush of color rose in her cheeks.

"I hope so, if Perceau doesn't lock me in the padded cell."

"I'll look forward to seeing you there, then."

The limited nature of the quasi-telepathy existing between humans and their alices on Drego might, in these circumstances, be not so displeasing a hindrance as he had at first surmised. Olive Cameron, now. . . . How Sinbad would be laughing at him; how Boris would have guffawed!

Although, to be sure, no one here on Ashramdrego was as yet fully conversant with all the ramifications of their alices' love lives. None had been known to conceive. They were found living sedentary lives among the rows of geron bushes and brought into the Kriseman compound. There they waited, fed on simple food from the humans' kitchens, until a symbiont needed them. Wade had heard vaguely of the frantic rush in which the first tests and experiments had been held and the marvelous aptitude of these creatures—who had been called squoodles by the first human arrivals—for symbiosis.

For a few moments he debated the necessity of

25

going to see Dot-Dot Hedges. He knew he was fit and sane in himself, but Perceau had sounded strict and authoritative. Wade had no desire to stir up avoidable trouble. He walked quietly back to the CT Building, concretely stark in the afternoon light.

He liked the mood of the base. Even Perceau and his military posture could be tolerated amongst a company of good fellows and girls. They were here to do a good job, to grow geron bushes—that was Baron w'Prortal's department—and to process gerontidril—that was Alexander Lokoja's department—from the harvest—that was everybody's department, and everyone got on with everyone else. Despite the tragedies, one of which had resulted in Wade's application for employment with the Kriseman Corporation bringing him here, a sense of lightness and good-natured fun sparkled in this Kriseman Corporation Headquarters.

The tearing sound of a ship lowering on power through atmosphere to the surface brought his head up to scan the glowing afternoon sky. The arrival of spaceships on Altimus had been, as here on Drego, enough of an event to break the day's routine. Knowing he would see nothing he yet looked until the shredded sound dwindled and died out on the spacefield.

Others had been watching too and now Eva Vetri scuttled past, her brown face alive with excitement.

"That's Trujillo now!" she said unnecessarily. "Now the party can start. I need a good orgy like crazy."

"They've got to be processed first," said Wade, a little too dryly. "The sun will be down before they're all out of the CT Building."

"Spoilsport!" she pouted at him. "I've cleared my outstanding work. Have you?"

He'd forgotten that routine inquiry at the Star House computer. Now he smiled easily.

"I had a little run in with a game of marbles."

"So it was you!" She laughed, as Olive Cameron had only smiled. "I might have known." She began to walk off, still laughing, flaunting her hips, then turned to say: "I still don't figure out how you handled the GBM without a file—"

But Wade walked quickly way. He'd have to be more careful in future. His main work would begin only when he processed the symb-socketeers for the harvest.

Thinking like that, relaxing, warm with the new fresh feelings of friendliness toward these people of the Kriseman Corporation growing and processing gerontidril, Matthew Wade walked pleasantly back to the CT Building to see Doctor Dot-Dot Hedges. He looked forward to the ball this evening. He'd have to dance with Olive Cameron, and Eva Vetri, too; but he knew with an unwanted dismayed feeling that the one person he really wished to dance with probably would do no more than smile and pass on. Doctor Marian Anstee would almost certainly be otherwise engaged.

He'd face that tonight. He flicked his camouflage cape neatly around his back. Ever since the work-leisure equations had been formulated men and women in the galaxy had lived with their eyes open.

So it was that the excited chatter and laughter of the group of people from the ship enhanced his own mood as they debouched from the sealed corridor from the spacefield. He saw bright clothes, quick gestures, faces of many colors, much brilliant jewelry. He received the impression of a circus troupe bearing down on him. He started to smile —and the smile remained, a petrified grimace on his abruptly haggard face.

Among that brilliant assembly, among but not of them, paced a tall man wearing a deep blue cloak, its hood drawn forward in a cowl. Around his waist he wore a silver chain.

Instantly, in recognizing the man as a bailiff from Altimus, Wade recognized that his fellow coords of Altimus in their constant search for him had once more found him.

The shock drove sickness into his guts. His uncoordinated mind palpitated with conscious fear. Quickly he stepped into the shadow of an alcove.

III

MATTHEW WADE COWERED in the alcove.

Altimus. . . .

They would never relent, never abandon this relentless search for him. Relentlessness, yes, indeed, that fairly described the coords of Altimus and C.I.D.G.

The floodgates of memory spilled their painful detritus into his mind. He remembered the first time the bailiffs and the tipstaffs had caught up with him after his escape.

That had been on a world vastly different from this one, on the open world of Tiberious where the malingerers and malcontents of the galaxy forgathered. He had in his naivety thought it offered the perfect haven.

In company with Brother Stanley he had taken off from Altimus and after a few self-conscious and deprecatory maneuvers and trail-hiding evolutions in space they had made planetfall on Tiberious. He had often wondered why the extra letter O had been added. A mark of exclamation, truly, a mark of zero.

He could feel the pulse of the ship's power dying, the tremble along her fabric dwindling. He could hear Brother Stanley chuckling, a stout, swarthy man with fierce eyes and overlarge hands and a zest for the good things of life that Altimus had failed to offer him. Not a coord, not that; but a superlatively efficient computer man, Brother Stanley had no doubts that they had done the right thing, saw no problems in their future.

"Snap out of it, Mat! By Astir! We've done it. We're here, on Tiberious, and we can soon land snip jobs as computer men." He rubbed his stomach complacently. "Now we can start to live it up."

Wade roused himself. "Yes, Stan. You're right, of course—"

"Of course I'm right. And I need to examine the birds on this little paradise. That's what you need—"

Wade broke the conversation by thumbing the airlock open. Together they went down the ramp onto Tiberious.

Less than two weeks later the myth had collapsed.

"Drink up, Mat! Have fun!"

Wade sipped his benze-whis, disliking the stuff, but willing to follow Stanley's lead. Around them the bar tinkled away tinnily, garish lights, chrome, laughter, smell, noise combining to paste a facsimile of enjoyment over the scene. Brother Stanley was chatting up two girls. They giggled. The one with blonde hair and green eyes and pimples kept ogling Wade and rubbing her nyloned leg against him under the table. He forced himself to keep his leg in position. How did he know how to react with normal people?

Brother Stanley knew. But then, Brother Stanley was not a coord.

"Hey, Gladys, I'm the best goddam computer man this side of Alpha Centauri—hell, this side of old Earth herself!"

"You ever been to Earth, Stan?"

He huffed himself up, his swarthy face grinning, a gold filling glinting.

"Naw. But I'll get around to it." He winked. "Maybe even take you along for the ride, Gladys. Hey?"

She simpered back. She must have heard that story a hundred times.

Gladys was the one wearing leotards that would have been too tight on a girl three-quarters her size. She giggled again and drank the colored water in her glass. Wade watched all this with the academic knowledge and removed interest of the trained observer.

"They're just a bunch of bums on this hick planet," Brother Stanley went on, drinking, laughing, playing to the gallery. He did not notice the two men clad in blue who entered quietly, moving like wraiths; men with tight trousers and dark blue shirts; men with sallow blank faces with eyes like coals. But Matthew Wade saw them.

His drink spilled across the formica tabletop.

"Hey! Stupe! You sozzled or sump'n?"

"Stan! Look!"

Brother Stanley looked. He dropped his full glass. "Hell!"

The table crashed over. Gladys squealed and Wade's girl screamed as benze-whis cascaded into her lap.

Shouts and a fight broke out at once at the adjoining table as Stanley knocked that flying, too. A fist glance off his lowered head. He swept his own hamlike fist out, brushing aside opposition, charging for the rear door to the cloakrooms. Wade just sat there, numbed.

The rear door opened. A man stood there, a tall gaunt man all in deep royal blue, the cloak swathing him to his heels, the hood thrown back. The silver belt girthing his waist glittered. The bailiff took one white hand from the wide sleeve of the blue robe beneath the cloak. He held the hand up, palm out, fingers flat, a halt sign unmistakable throughout the human galaxy.

Brother Stanley skidded, backpedaling, fighting to stay on his feet. He slammed into a table, spilled drinks and girls every which way, vaulted across the debris, charged headlong for a window.

Bedlam broke out.

Gladys and Wade's girl crashed into each other as they hit the floor. They sheltered beneath the rocking table. Benze-whis dripped onto their tatty finery.

Wade stood up.

31

A man tried to knock him down and automatically he swayed away from the blow, making no attempt to strike back.

Brother Stanley took most of the window frame with him garlanding his neck. Glass popped and shattered. The two tipstaffs, their blue uniforms tight and menacing, started after him.

The bailiff, his royal blue cloak swirling, advanced.

Not the bailiff, not the tipstaffs, not Brother Stanley had spoken. Words were unnecessary here.

The girls, between their screaming, took thought for Wade, isolated like some abandoned pharos amid the confusion.

. "Hey, Mat! Get your fool head down!"

Their concern touched him. He roused himself.

The two tipstaffs, lithe, agile men, raced after Brother Stanley. The bailiff, whose gaunt, chalk-white face and demeanor of absolute integrity amid any indescribable scenes of confusion struck a chill into Wade, moved forward.

Glasses and bottles flew. Shouts rose. Men twisted in combat, striking and being struck, not knowing or caring who had started the fight or why it was being fought but merely joying in the brute strength of their blows. Avoiding a collapsing pair of men like marionettes in their awkward conflict, Wade strode rapidly through the melee. To run now would be disastrous.

"Mat! You Astir-forsaken nit! Get down!"

He ignored the blonde girl, whose nylons now were laddered and ruined. He ducked a flying bottle. It smashed into the sweating face of a man trying to brain him with an upraised chair.

Brother Stanley, for the moment, had drawn the bloodhounds from Altimus away. There were perhaps two minutes in which to act.

He passed rapidly between contorting bodies and the steady crashings of bottles and glasses toward the cloakroom door and the rear exit, now left open as a bolthole by the bailiff.

A long thin tentacle of coiled beryl-steel caught his bicep. He swung around.

A lensed metal face atop a chunky robot body glared single-mindedly at him.

"You have not settled your bill, sir. Please do not leave until you have paid."

"I don't have time right now."

"My function as assistant to the barkeep is to insure you pay your reckoning, sir. Please do not leave until you have paid."

The bailiff had joined the two tipstaffs who were vaulting agilely through the Stanley-smashed window.

"Look," said Wade with desperate ingenuity. "I'm only going to the cloakroom—"

"I'm afraid that is a story I hear many times during my periods of duty. I must ask you to settle your reckoning before leaving."

The bailiff was turning to scan the room. Wade dug a hasty fist into his pocket, came up with a few moldy coins.

"This is all I have on my person. My friend had our money. So far we have not obtained jobs—"

The robot's eye lenses sparkled dangerously.

"Out of a job and you partake of my employer's refreshments! I must ask you to accompany me to—"

Wade ducked his head as the icy gaze of the

bailiff swept across the room. He cowered down behind the robot who turned clankingly, saying menacingly: "That will do you no good, sir. No good at all. Please accompany me to—"

Wade grasped the tentacle in his right hand and pulled. He felt the immediate constriction on his arm and then his cheap coat sleeve split. For just a moment the tentacle slid. With a violent apocalyptic heave, Wade snatched his arm free. He kicked the robot in the metal canister body, dodged a flailing sweep of tentacle and rushed through the door.

"You have not settled your bill, sir, you will please accompany me to—"

The swing door slammed back across the other, the noise blotting out the robot's complaining voice. Now Wade would never know where he was to have accompanied the robot.

Through the rear door in a blur of speed Matthew Wade raced in a mock shadowing of youthful races along the water meadows, dodging the cows and sheep. Brilliant splashing light cascaded about him, multicolored and harsh, vibrant, demanding, pouring from the commercial signs and advertisements along this pleasure boulevard of Tiberious. He blinked. Sounds of shouting and the harsh slam of boots on paving drew his attention toward the alley.

Surely Stan must have run off by now?

But no. Here he came, leaping like a goaded goat, springing out of the alley and flying up the street, cannoning into people, rebounding, haring on.

Wade made a single startled step forward.

The two tipstaffs appeared, running evenly, their

arms like pistons, their chests moving in rhythm, untroubled by wind. They turned with matching velocity and shot off after Brother Stan.

A profound and scalding sense of responsibility for the recalcitrant Stan made Matthew Wade move after them.

He wanted with desperate fear to run away and hide himself in this flamboyant city. That he could not abandon his ruffianly if simple comrade rankled within him like a slur upon his sanity. His breath panted thickly. He wasn't in as good shape as he ought to be.

No sign of the bailiff meant merely that that devious official would be off hatching further schemes. The very coldness and remoteness of the bailiffs had always, even when he was a ranking coord, troubled Wade and had been instrumental in his final decision to abscond.

People just picking themselves up after the tempestuous passage of Brother Stanley were knocked flying again by the two tipstaffs in full cry. By the time Wade charged up to them they were in no mood to be knocked down again. He had to duck and weave and dodge to get through.

The indignity of this whole senseless series of actions annoyed and depressed Wade. This, surely, was not what should have been meted out to him when the bailiff had first called on his father and mother?

The constant streams of traffic whirling by prevented Brother Stanley from seeking escape to the side; like a chip of pinewood gleaming yellow in a millrace, he was forced to plunge straight ahead.

A clicking, clanking noise clopped after Wade.

Away down the street hared Brother Stanley. After him in full cry leaped the two tipstaffs. After them pounded Wade. And after Wade galloped the shiny form of the robot, menacingly coiling and uncoiling its tentacles and flashing lights on and off.

They made quite a notable procession.

"Oh, no!" groaned Wade, puffing along. "All the cupidity of man transferred to an insensate machine!"

Ahead, the branching silver of the monorails glinted against the neon-tinted night, cars sweeping and swooping like scintillating teardrops sliding down the metal cheeks of petrified giants. The traffic hauled up here. Between two hovercars Brother Stanley flung himself across the pavement and, like a scuttling beetle, headed for the shadows of the monorail. Immaculately in step, vigorous and unstoppable, the two tipstaffs executed a smart turn and burrowed through the traffic after Stan.

Wondering what the hell good he was doing, Matthew Wade followed.

Common sense—the way ordinary mortals of the galaxy operated—dictated that he complete a diametric turn and take off in the opposite direction. He'd deal with the rapacious robot all right.

Passersby stopped to listen, charmed by the exhibition. The robot's scratchy voice kept on chinkling out.

"Please pay your bill, sir. Please accompany me to—" Again that hiatus as the destination of the robot was obliterated by the angry howl of a car horn. "You haven't settled your reckoning, sir." Then as Wade ran sturdily on down into the monorail arches' shadows, surprisingly: "You rotten welcher!"

That stung Wade.

"So I am!" he threw over his shoulder, not stopping running, red in the face and with laboring lungs. "So you try to catch me, you perambulating hunk of ironmongery!"

"Sir, I am impervious to abuse, not comprehending the finer nuances of insult."

"Go boil your head!"

For Wade had lost sight of the tipstaffs there among the creeping shadows and the gonging echoes from the cars above. He searched, knowing that he sought those who would arrest him, and yet unable not to search because—because, hell, it was good old Brother Stan, wasn't it?

A shaft of lurid crimson light fell from an angled sign located to impinge on the gaze of monorail passengers. In that ruby glow Wade caught a furtive glimpse of movement. Stan emerged, looking cautiously around.

About to shout to him, Wade saw the two tipstaffs appear about twenty-five yards to Stan's rear. Two blue shadows purpled in the ruby radiance, they crept nearer.

At that moment, caught in hideous indecision, Wade felt the avaricious tentacle of the robot on his shoulder.

"Get off, you hunk of machinery!" he yelped, startled. And then: "Look! There they are, those two men in blue. They've got the money. They'll pay the reckoning."

Wade imagined in that metal chest cogs whirring, currents flowing, transistors transisting. The robot focused his eye lenses.

"I will ask them for the money, sir," he chirruped at last. "Please be good enough to remain here."

What happened then could not have been foreseen, not, Wade considered somberly, even by a fully linked up coord such as he had once been.

The two tipstaffs, almost ready to pounce upon Stanley, swiveled as the robot ran up to them, flashing his lights and flailing his tentacles. What they thought Wade couldn't know at that time; what Stanley thought, as he swiveled about and shouted, that, too, Wade couldn't know. He saw what happened.

One tipstaff produced a gun and vaporized the robot.

The other cut down Stanley as he ran, left him an oozing puddle on the cold concrete of the road.

Wade turned away. The nausea rose in him. He tasted the vile stink of vomit in his mouth. He clenched his jaws. He stumbled off into the darkness, blindly.

IV

For a flashing instant as Matthew Wade watched Kolok Trujillo and his party chattering and gesticulating gaily on their way to the symbiosis theater, with the gaunt blue-clad form of the bailiff from Altimus among them, he shuddered back from the demented gulf of his memories to a hollow tenet of weak-minded religious converts. Out of a garbled belief in original sin they wrote that if a man practiced evil it must mean that he saw there was good, in the absolutes of those terms. It had seemed to Wade that these writers failed to grasp the essential truth of what they preached; that in seeing evil but practicing good a man fulfills himself in every way. Faulty religious beliefs had produced far more than their fair share of misery in the galaxy.

From the shadows he watched that gaudy party of cosmopolitan sophisticates. The bailiff stood out among them like the avenging finger of God. Even, he saw with a faint and sad echo of his old professionalism, the yellow-robed form of a regnant —he could not see at this distance to which Order the regnant belonged—looked not out of place among the vivacious throng. The Regnancy tried to hold themselves as the prior mystic Order of the galaxy; to a coord they were another of the small fry.

Clearly, he had failed Brother Stanley.

If even by his own death he could have swayed the event, then surely as a human being he should have given his life. Brother Stanley had been killed because he had absconded from Altimus. Oh, yes, the rapacious robot had triggered the final tragedy. There was always a reasoned excuse to hand.

He shook himself out of that fit of masochistic self-indulgence. Brother Stanley was dead. If he didn't want to join him, he would have to steer clear of the bailiff. And yet how, here on Ashramdrego with no dark-shadowed monorails, could that be done?

The perfect excuse existed for him now not to have seen Dot-Dot Hedges. At once he retraced his steps and left the CT Building. The level rays of the sun showed the afternoon as being nearly spent and, a revulsion for his office seizing him, he went off toward the compound bar. The base boasted more than one bar but he had in his short time here come to prefer the Split Infinitive. Its quietness gave one time to contemplate the sins of the galaxy, and its wines the lucidity with which to correct them.

The way lay past the military office. A mock castle front covered the entrance with a three-dimensional projection filming away, showing a smartly attired sentry pacing up and down. At first Wade had dodged out of its way. Now he simply walked straight on and, for an instant, his shirt became a writhing pattern of striding arms and legs, webbing belts, weapons and steel helmets. Then the projected sentry marched stolidly on and Wade resumed his normal coloration.

A second uniformed figure appeared in the doorway, hastily buckling on an antigrav pack and a weapons bet. This one was real flesh and blood.

"Hey, you—what's-your-name, c'mere!"

Wade ignored all such remarks from habit.

"You! The guy with the camouflage cape! C'mere!"

As there was no one else on the walk, everyone presumably having gone to clean and titivate for the evening's entertainment, and as Wade did indisputably possess a Samian camouflage cape, he conceded that the uncouth warrior must be addressing none other than Matthew Wade.

He put this into words as politely as he could.

The young man's face, which had been contorted into a tight, highly colored knot, broke into a delighted smile.

"I'm sorry if I sounded curt, old man. But there's a spot of'an emergency on and there's just nobody else about, not a jolly soul. So it's you and me, chum."

His fresh face and his cropped but shining hair, his scrubbed cheeks, his immaculate uniform, worn without the plastic imitation antique grenades, impressed Wade with the vision of a lolloping puppy, all tongue and feet, galumphing around a doting master.

"Emergency?"

"Too true. Over in Gamma Eleven. The confounded ruptors are stripping it down to twigs and bark."

"You," said Wade, falling into step with this impetuous young man and taking gingerly from him the proffered weapons belt, "must be the D.D.O."

"'sright. The D.O. is tied up in the CT Building right now. Sorry; but I don't know you."

Wade smiled. "I've only been here six days and I believe you've—"

"I've been over beyond the Fractured Hills. Tough country. The ruptors over there are playing up like old Harry, too. Can't think what's got into the beasts lately." He increased speed. "There seems to be millions more of the dratted things these days, too." They fairly ran into the flier park.

"I'm Matthew Wade," said Wade, following the deputy defense officer up into the cockpit of a three-place flier.

"I'm Tom Martin. I just get back and hear there's a ball on for Kolok Trujillo and then—bingo!—I'm off again. It's all go."

"It's all go," agreed Wade gravely.

Martin sat beside the driver while Wade took

41

the third seat to the rear. The driver, a blocky sergeant with a nearly black alice, a hard face and eyes that looked meanly out upon a circumscribed world, took the flier up at once. Wade sat uncomfortably. At least, this emergency took him away from the headquarters and the bailiff.

Below them in the fading light the even rows of geron bushes broke the plantations into reticulations of light and shade. Unendingly they stretched away on every side, broken only by the now fully visible enclosure of the Kriseman Corporation Headquarters compound. They looked somehow sentient in a positive sense, close-breasted against the ground, breaking with dapples of green blackness and silver brightness in row after row, parallel, diagonal, continually forming and reforming fresh open avenues of vision as the flier spun down the perspectives.

"They told me I'd grow younger working around them," nodded the sergeant, indicating the geron bushes in general. "Can't say as I've noticed any extra virility."

Martin chuckled.

"I suppose that's why you volunteered to come to Ashramdrego and wear an alice, hey, sar'nt?"

Wade killed his smile. The sergeant could see him in the rear view mirror and Wade just wasn't sure how a man woud react. . . .

"Sure, and why not? If sniffing a few bushes is gonna set me up for the birds, who am I to grumble?"

"I just wonder," said Martin with a strange lilting chuckle, "what old Jean Baptiste Poquelin would have made of everyone rushing to Ashram-drego—"

"Probably," said Wade, without thinking, "he'd say: 'What the devil did they go in the galley for?' "

"Whassat?" asked the sergeant, swinging the flier toward a cleft in the nearing hills.

Tom Martin turned right around in the seat, gently pushing his alice aside to gain a better view of Wade. He lifted his eyebrows.

"The sergeant's no Scapin," he said, and then waited, obviously expecting a retort.

Wade let his smile grow.

"I'm new around here, remember, but I'd guess that the director, Silas Sternmire, might make a passable Harpagon."

The D.D.O. positively beamed.

"A fellow Molièreist! I say, old man, this is great!"

Martin swiveled his seat fully around now. "I'm researching the very real connection between Plautus, Molière and Strathan, after all, there's just about the same time interval between them."

"Yes, but between Plautus and Molière you had the Dark Ages."

"Sure. You mean that the influence was direct. but there'd been the TEST war just before Strathan and that carved great chunks out of culture."

"Not the same thing." Wade felt absolutely no surprise or inappropriateness in flying off to battle gigantic winged pests and discussing important subjects like the relationship of the matters of Comedy. "And Strathan had everything working for him. Plautus was probably a slave, and Jean Baptiste, well now, look at the trouble Tartuffe landed him in."

"Oh, I'll grant you that. My researches are getting along nicely, and I've even had to include Terence." Martin settled down to what was his obviously abiding passion. Wade glanced ahead and saw the nearness of the hills, wildly green and yellow in the dying light, the reds leached out and lying like streaks of blood along the slopes. The geron bushes made no attempt to climb those inhospitable tracts.

"Coming up, sir," grunted the sergeant, cutting Martin off in mid-flight about Monsieur Jourdain and people he knew back home.

"Oh, bother," sighed the D.D.O. "I suppose I'll learn to be a soldier one day; but right now I want to talk about the role of slave and robot with you, old man."

"Any time," said Wade. "I'll be happy."

Martin revolved his seat and faced forward as the flier plunged down from the pass over the ferocious natural vegetation and out over the man-ordered rows of geron bushes.

"The eepees have been knocked out again." The tart exasperation coarsened Martin's voice.

"These great overgrown bumblebees have a clout on 'em sir." The sergeant swung the flier down headlong. "They gang up on the eepees. I've seen 'em."

Over every plantation of the continent, small in number as yet but growing every planting time, guardian electroplasms kept watch and ward. Perambulating electronic scarecrows, manifestly, they had failed to scare.

Wade snatched a glimpse of a shining form crumpled like discarded tinfoil.

Then he saw along a straight run of geron bushes.

From the far end a commotion began. Leaves spun into the air. Tossed, curling, spinning, they showered up from a point that chewed its way along the row. It was like a circular saw ripping through a long pine log with the chippings and dust screeching up and out behind it.

The flier reversed, descended and matched speeds with the ruptor. Martin pushed his gun through the opened canopy and fired. The ruptor abruptly nosed down and slid into the dirt, spraying leaves and twigs and gouts of earth.

"Have to use explosive projectile weapons, at the moment," grunted the D.D.O. "Vaporizers would destroy the crop, too."

"There's another," snapped the sergeant.

The flier darted across. The gun flared. The ruptor nosedived into the bushes.

"Every time they do that our bonus on the harvest takes a nose dive, too," grumbled the sergeant.

Now Wade could see other rows of geron bushes being systematically stripped. He could not, as yet, clearly perceive the ruptors themselves. They moved fast. From one end of a row they would hurl themselves to the other in what at first seemed a dead straight run, but which, on closer inspection, revealed itself to be a species of high-jinking dips and rises, of swerves, of duckings and inexplicable haltings, all carried out so rapidly that only the most penetrating gaze could capture the variations. No pattern appeared. The strange cavortings in the direct line of flight seemed completely random.

Tom Martin kept firing with a steadiness of aim that Wade found unsettling.

"Come on, man, cut some of them down! That's what you're here for!"

Wade lifted his gun. All he knew about guns was that you pointed them and pulled the trigger. He pointed it in the general direction of a ruptor, pulled the trigger and blew a geron bush out of the ground.

"By Astir! Can't you shoot straighter than that?"

"I'm a little, uh, out of practice."

A shell from Martin's gun exploded directly beneath a ruptor, which shot vertically into the air, trailing intestines, turned over, smacked into the ground.

"There are at least fifty of the things. Sar'nt, get a message back. We'll need help."

The sergeant began talking into the microphone of his radio. Martin carried on shooting. Feeling unclean, Wade tried to hit a ruptor. The sun stroked shadows longer and longer.

"Sar'nt Goudsmit! Hand over the controls to Wade; start shooting yourself. Wade—you can handle a flier, I suppose?"

Relieved, not at all ashamed, Wade nodded. He crabbed awkwardly up from his seat. The sergeant slid his canopy window wide open and drew his gun. The flier, for a moment, sped along straight and true on its automatic pilot.

Three or four ruptors left off cropping the geron bushes. They swarmed up in a knot. One of them exploded into a bright gout of flame and blood, then the others turned directly onto a collision course with the flier.

"They're after us now!" yelled Martin. He fired again and missed.

Wade thought of the crumpled metal form of the eepee.

Lon Chaney, his camouflage coat, rippled himself up into a long tight ribbon and pressed hard up against Wade, gripping tightly with his sixteen limbs. There was no need of telepathic communication now to tell the cloak to hold on and expect trouble.

Sinbad hiccuped. "Take it gently, Sinbad," Wade symbed. "We'll be all right."

The response pattern formed in his mind with a noticeable and disturbing lack of all giggle overtones; the alice didn't like this. Wade had noticed that all three alices had shown unmistakable symptoms of nervousness the moment they'd contacted the ruptors.

He humped himself up ready to move forward and take over the driving position.

Martin was still shooting, shooting and missing as the remaining ruptors bored on in a jinking, weaving confusing flight.

Sergeant Goudsmit leveled his gun. He fired once.

The leading ruptor dissolved in smoke and exploded flesh. The second ruptor screamed in through the debris, its body passing scant inches above the canopy. Its sting projecting below and ahead of its body drove in through the opened canopy, pierced in a spouting of blood and brain through the sergeant's head, snicked back like a disengaged cavalry lance. It struck the opened canopy a third of its length from the root and snapped straight. Then it was gone.

Sergeant Goudsmit collapsed back into his seat, tripping open the automatic pilot, slumping down

over the controls. Blood and brains spattered the
canopy.

Martin shouted once, a deep vicious curse, and
tried to shove the body away from the controls. The
flier pitched over. It started down.

Wade reached forward, grabbed the sergeant's collar feeling the wet slickness there, heaved back.
Martin was trying to force his hand in between the
dead man and the controls. The ground rushed up.

"Pull him, Wade—*pull him!*"

Wade heaved. The body inched up, jammed
against controls and seat, as unyielding and as awkward as a hop pocket caught under a tractor's
wheels. Wade took a deep breath, gripped and
pulled. The body rippled. It started to come up
and Martin shoved both hands at the controls.
Then the uniform collar riped off and Wade tumbled back into the seat tangled up with the sergeant's black alice. The body slopped forward onto Martin. The flier pitched into the ground.

V

THE FLIER SCRAPED through the geron bushes for
two hundred yards, falling to pieces all the way.

The two men still alive did not lose consciousness.

Buffeted and banged about, Wade at last realized the nightmare ride had ceased. They were
down. Dust and stripped geron leaves floated
downwind in a plume signaling their destruction.

Martin and Wade sat there. Broken thoughts

floated through Wade's dizzied mind: relief at still being alive gave him now only a calm warm glow that could not, as yet, blank off the horror of that traumatic crashing moment.

Martin breathed in, breathed out, hefted his gun and spat.

"The things will be after us now. Get under the flier, Wade. And for the sake of Blind Astir—shoot straight!"

They scrambled out of the wreckage. Wade felt pain shooting through his shoulders and shook himself roughly, annoyed. Sinbad stirred. No sign remained of dead Sergeant Goudsmit's black alice. Come to think of it, as Wade slid into the crumbly loam and brought his gun up, he hadn't noticed Silas Sternmire's alice take off. The local life support systems had a way of making themselves scarce, it seemed.

With his usual proficient anticipation, Lon Chaney adapted to his surroundings, the chromatophores covering his skin changing color to blend in with the brown and green of the geron-leaved ground.

"A camouflage cloak is just about what the doctor ordered now, Wade. I wish I had one.

Martin chopped off Wade's reply by firing and sending a ruptor spiraling into the dirt, shedding gauzy wings. This close up to the ruptors in full action, buzzing with energy and vitality, Wade reacted afresh to their size and venom. The glass-cased specimens back in the administration building had not prepared him for the sheer ferocity of the living animal.

He took a few potshots and succeeded in hitting

the fourth target. The wrecked flier gonged as prob-ing stings glanced off its shattered metal.

"We can't last much longer at this rate," snapped Martin. He reloaded as he spoke. The look on his face worried Wade.

Now a continuous attack developed. Ruptor after ruptor hurled itself down on them. Dirt gouted into the poisonous air as sting after sting scraped along the ground seeking to impale the humans crouching beneath the scrap of cover.

The ruptor's pincers, when firmly closed together, presented a formidable weapon, capable of thrust-ing through thin dural, capable of impaling a hu-man being as a lepidopterist imales a moth on a specimen pin.

The battle roared on. Dust and sweat caked Wade's strained face. The gun grew hot in his hand. Continually, now, Martin searched the sky for sign of rescue. But the sky returned only the buzzing animosity of the ruptors.

A pattern from Sinbad formed in his mind. Through the overriding apprehension a pleasure line inti-mated a return to the old giggle muscles in full play. Something in this ghastly situation appealed to his alice.

The wrecked flier lay in a dusty, leaf-strewn cir-cle of dead ruptors and uprooted geron bushes. The light at last began to fade. In the encroaching shadows the ruptors could put in their attacks with greater immunity, only being fired on at the last moment.

Soon, the last moment would be too late.

In the phantasmic shifting of purple shadows

the ruptors drew off. Miraculously, there grew a breathing space.

"Luis Perceau wants to kill off all the ruptors with a hormone dust." Wade spoke slowly, with care.

Martin laughed with a harshness bordering on a state of mind Wade did not relish.

"I've been against that policy. Too vicious, atavistic, and most of the base agreed with me. It might have unforeseen repercussions." He stared out, his young face grimed and bedraggled like an urchin's. "But now I think I've changed my mind."

"If the citizens of the galaxy demand longer life spans, then they must pay the price—even if it means killing off a species. Astir knows, mankind has killed off enough animals in his time. . . ." Wade waited. The young man only grunted. "There are rewards for which the conscience will bargain."

"You didn't come here, then, because the geron bushes grow on Drego?" Martin did not sound the same man who had so blithely discussed Plautus and Molière.

"I came because when I applied for a job with the Kriseman Corporation I was assigned here. You' had troubles—a lot of staff died—I know—"

"Too right, we'd had troubles. We've still got troubles."

"What are the ruptors waiting for? Perhaps they don't like nighttime. Maybe they've gone."

Martin shook his head. His skin around his mouth looked mummified. "No. The light hasn't all gone, anyway. They'll be back—"

In the next instant they were back, flying in solid wedges of destruction that smashed deafeningly into the flier, rocking it, sending showers of dust flying.

Martin began firing, half-blindly, great spurts of lurid flame in the dusk. Wade joined in. The flier rolled. Caught in a concentration of movement it tipped, snagged a geron bush, dragged it free of the ground and rolled right over.

Martin rolled flat after it, beating off the pointed lances that darted at him. Wade triggered a long burst and then squirmed afer Matrin. Lon Chaney, rippling, did his job, covering Wade. A lance snicked into the ground by Martin's head, thumping him aside. The beast's body exploded as Wade fired with the precision of desperation. Martin slumped. Wade stopped firing and the ruptors drew off. Darkness dropped with the last finality.

Breathing raspingly, Sinbad symbed a pattern of alarm.

"I think they've gone, Sinbad," symbed Wade. "Just keep still."

After a few moments during which he remained like a dead man, Wade crawled laboriously across to Martin. He saw the young man's body with eyes adjusting to the dimness. Something moved around his shoulders. A furry form, indistinct, sluggish, rippled.

Without thought, flinging himself forward, Wade fell across the D.D.O.'s body. He saw the alice crawl under a geron bush. Then he had clamped his mouth to Martin's mouth. He pinched the man's nose savagely between finger and thumb. Around them the poisonous gases rolled. He breathed in through his nose and then out through his mouth, blowing into Martin's mouth. He dared not take his own mouth away for an instant. Lying sprawled, uncomfortable, he administered the kiss of life and hoped that he was not too late.

His Samian camouflage cloak undulated and adjusted himself to both Wade and Martin, tucking his legs in, neatly packaging them whilst his cromatophores dutifully aped the color of their surroundings. Lon Chaney, as ever, was earning his keep.

Martin tried to move, weakly stirring a hand, a leg. His lips writhed. Wade funneled his own hand around their joined mouths. He pinched hard down with the other hand on Martin's nostrils. If Martin, dazed, tried to heave off this body pressing him down, this limpet affixed to his mouth, he'd breathe once and be dead.

As it was, Wade didn't like to think what the noxious atmosphere was doing to other parts of the D.D.O.'s anatomy without the symbiotic relationship of his and his alice's bloodstreams.

He had no idea how long he could keep this up. Sinbad symbed a pattern of reassurance, an understanding of the problem, that he was now supporting four lives and, like a refrigerator in the tropics, a giggle note of relief that the ruptors had gone. Wade continued to blow air his lungs had mechanically provided but that Sinbad had processed through their conjoined bloodstreams into Martin's mouth.

Flecks spun before his staring gaze. He could feel the blood—the vital blood—pounding in his eardrums. His chest hurt. He dared not move for fear a spasm from the dazed D.D.O. would dislodge him. Cramped, desperate, enduring, Matthew Wade held on.

Martin's exhalations from his nostrils, rigidly controlled by Wade's pinching and constricting fingers, presented a hazard he could only pray he could control. Better for Martin to choke up a bit on a recoil of air than to expel and then begin to breathe in.

How long, Wade wondered, blackness ringing his consciousness, numbness beginning in his jaw and throat, how long? He blinked and blinked again, deliberately. A geron leaf blew by, indistinct in the dimness but close enough for him to make out its spear shape, its thick juicy veins, its richness of hue blanketed by dusk. A yellow ovoid showed on the underside of the leaf. The yellow presented a dull whitish patch, irregular, but Wade knew enough of his own powers of observation as a coord to know what his senses told him he saw.

The leaf blew by. Wade breathed and waited.

Dust irritated in his eyes, gritted under the lids. He did not release a hand to clear the irritation. He waited.

Leaves pattered against his body. He recalled other days of autumn when leaves had spiraled in red gold from tall trees, when the fall gilded golden flames across a continent, when the air tasted of wine. Now was no time to relapse into that aching bed of memory. Now he must concentrate all his being on doing what he had to do, for the only reason he could see for existence, in his responsibility to this unhappy, bewildered young man whose life balanced on an alien's lung capacity.

When at last actinic lights blazed in a circle over him and the wash of a flier beat down the geron leaves and cascaded whorls of dust, Matthew Wade had reached very nearly the end of his endurance. Hands lifted him and Martin. A lung slipped its plastic oxygen-nitrogen safety over Martin's face. Wade flopped back and tried to find the strength to smile.

His lips were bloodless. His whole face was stiff like gutta-percha. His body ached as though beaten with a lathi.

Lights flashed in his eyes. He saw faces, bending over him. He was lifted, carried to the flier, put down. Long before the flier reached the compound Wade was asleep.

VI

"If ever," said Doctor Marian Anstee, "the value of symbiosis for planetary development was in doubt, your experiences last night would have convinced even the most recalcitrant. If you'd been in space suits with a few bottles of oxygen between you, you'd be dead now."

"Good old Sinbad," said Wade, and symbed the same to his alice, who hiccuped vulgarly in response.

"I owe you my life, Mat," said Martin. He looked very pale, green almost, and gaunt with a new knowledge.

"To Sinbad and to Lon Chaney. As soon as my cloak covered us both the ruptors couldn't find us. That should give the biology boys a few thoughts."

They sat in the lounge of the hospital, comfortable, rested, ready for dinner. Wade had the uncomfortable feeling that Martin would never rid himself of that green-tinged, haunted look. He had almost regained his old high spirits.

Perceau said harshly: "I'm sorry, Tom, that we were so long reaching you." He scowled. "I'm having a few hides for that. It was that damn fool ball for Kolok Trujillo. I like my station to be run better than that—"

"Sergeant Goudsmit," said Martin, breathily. "The sting went right through his head—blood and brains everywhere—"

Doctor Dot-Dot Hedges cut him off, as he had each time the young D.D.O. had mentioned the sergeant's death.

"Dinner's almost ready," said Hedges. "Although what the dee-dot-dot-em cook's hashed up for us today I don't like to think. Sar'nt Goudsmit is dead, Tom. There's not a thing anyone can do about that, except bury him. It wasn't your fault. You did a good job."

"Sure—"

Marian Anstee put a slender hand on his shoulder, alongside his new alice. "Dot-Dot's right, Tom. Shall we eat?"

"Although," added Hedges. "That decamping alice dropped Tom right in the ess-dot-dot-tee and complicated the rest of it."

"That was the trouble before, wasn't it?" asked Wade, interested. "I mean, when you had that rash of deaths. The alices just, well, took off."

"They did." Marian Anstee held onto Martin as he rose slowly. "But that doesn't in any way negate the value of symbiosis."

"Huh," snorted Hedges. "I don't know why I'm

down here on Drego. I still have to be convinced these dee-dot-dot-em elices are—"

Marian Anstee flushed, the blood seeping crimson beneath her glistening skin. "I know all that, Dot-Dot! You know the speed we had to work at. Doctor Overbeck performed a miracle in locating and indoctrinating the squoodles. Kriseman wanted gerontidril for the galaxy. Aren't people entitled to an extension of their life span if we can provide it?"

. Doc Hedges spread his hands. "I'm not suggesting they aren't, confound it, Marian! All I'm saying is that there weren't enough tests run on the squoodles. You don't even have the faintest idea of their life cycle—"

Marian Anstee clutched Martin's arm and steered him to the door. "Doctor Overbeck is working on that right now." She went out, quickly, bending to Tom Martin.

Hedges sighed. "If she'd only think for herself instead of letting that mountebank Overbeck think for her! She regards him like a god!" He waved his arms about, getting up steam, caught Perceau's eye and, deflating, rumbled: "Oh, Luis, I know what you think of Overbeck. I say he's too cocky and sure of himself by half."

"He's just about the greatest doctor of symbiosis there is—"

"Doctor of eff-dot-dot-gee poppycock! I tell you, Luis, these alices we're wearing are a danger to us all!"

Luis Perceau's toughly brutal face showed contempt.

"Grow up, Dot-Dot! You're an M.D. You're our

local G.P. We need you, Astir knows! But when it comes to symbiosis let the experts handle it."

Hedges rumbled and huffed, then, with a lopsided smile at Wade, who had tactfully remained silent, he stumped out. A short, square man, with impatient eyes and excitable mannerisms, Dot-Dot Hedges in strange counterpoint contained the exact bedside manner, when necessary, of the finest doctors Earthside.

Perceau grunted. "If it wasn't for Doc Overbeck, none of us would be here. Doc Hedges just doesn't think."

"Still," said Wade, aware that he dealt with normal humans and amused at this sudden revelation of that, "there were those unexplained deaths due to the alices."

"Doc Overbeck knows what he's doing. Kriseman Corporation wouldn't have sent him here if he didn't. There isn't anyone better than him. Everyone knows that."

Turning to the door, Perceau finished: "And, Wade, thanks for saving young Tom Martin. You thought fast." He couldn't smile, not with that physiognomy; but his face crinkled up. He did not stroke his alice; of all the personnel on the base he was the only one Wade never saw luxuriously stroking his alice's fur like an animate netsuke. "You've been discharged from the meat shop as fully recovered. Let's go get dinner."

Wade followed the D.O. out of the hospital and across to the mess hall.

The folks wanted to make something of a hero of him.

Abruptly shy, abysmally unsure of how he should

react, he smiled and said "thank you" and then quickly sat down and spooned soup.

The ball for Kolok Trujillo had terminated convulsively in the news of the rescue. The delay would be explained, Perceau would see to that; but for Wade military discipline remained an unfathomable mystery. He had not encountered a disciplinary military problem when he'd been a coord on Altimus. He also learned another item of news that, despite his long training in impassivity, brought a fierce pleasure burning in his veins. The bailiff from Altimus who had come wth Trujillo's party had left. Some time during the ball he had been closeted with Silas Sternmire, and then had called down a ship waiting in orbit and had left about the affairs of the C.I.D.G.

That, at the least, presented no problem to an ex-coord. The bailiff had been negotiating for the continued, steady and preferential supply of gerontidril for all those on Altimus. That figured.

Wade felt the relief seep through him. Here on Ashramdrego he would not have to try to run as he had tried to run on Tiberious. Brother Stanley. Yes. . . .

The fresh insights to the problem and the conflicts festering beneath the surface of the base intrigued him as they whetted his appetite for more. The base was a happy place, yes; but, more than that, it shared with all of humanity's fabrications the seeds of dissension. It wouldn't have been human if it hadn't. There had been no dissensions on Altimus, not until Matthew Wade had upped and departed.

And yet, coords were of Homo sapiens stock, too.

He remembered once talking with a novelist, a breed of artist that had endured through the galactic expansion, in face of tridis, tellys, instafax shows and all the other sensory media. "You're not writing to morons," the novelist had said. "You coords who control the destinies of our progress—"

And Wade had been forced to interrupt, with a laugh, to say that coords merely coordinated interdisciplinary functions.

"That is what the original function was, yes," the novelist agreed. "But you cannot shake off your human origins. When I write, I write for adults. I don't have to explain everything. The reader grows in awareness as I want him to grow, so that he knows what he has to know at any given point in the story. Even with children you can take it for granted they're a lot tougher than we gave them credit for. If you don't follow what I'm talking about, then look to your own mental equipment; don't blame me as a writer."

"I agree," Wade smiled, thinking of Strathan—a ghostly echo from the future and of that fateful ride with Tom Martin—and watching Brother Pontifex with the wry smile of a man who is, all unknowingly, approaching the imminent edge of his own destruction. "As a novelist you came to Altimus expecting to find Lords of Creation and instead, as you see, we are merely ordinary men like yourself."

"Ordinary men, plus," said the novelist quickly.

"Agreed. But the plus is no miracle, no superhuman power. We are selected from parents who can have no knowledge that in their genes they carry this coordinated faculty."

"I've heard the selection process is stringent. But

I'd guess you'd find it hard to act naturally among ordinary people of the galaxy."

Here in the mess hall of the Kriseman Corporation Headquarters compound on Ashramdrego, Matthew Wade could vouch for the truth of that.

Looking back he remembered that the novelist had been the only man, out of statesmen, businessmen, soldiers, spacefarers, divines, scientists who had spoken to the coords not only with understanding and equality but as though they were really human.

Eva Vetri touched his arm with the tips of her fingers, her brown, petite face laughing and mocking.

"You're quite a guy, Mat."

"Uh—"

Others crowded around us as the meal finished. Wade stood up, feeling more of a fool than he had since the day he'd worn fancy dress to a formal party; and that had been—oh, when he thought he was growing up, just before the bailiff had come and hauled him off to Altimus.

Eventually, when he'd managed to shake off the admiring throng, he wandered along to the administration building. He stood in the dimness a moment, then clicked on the overheads. Light fell across the glass case and the three dead ruptors.

He stared at them.

Limp, dead, dull, their burnished colors of life faded, they bore little resemblance to the vivid darting horrors that had tried to spear and degut him.

He took from his pocket a small yellow ovoid he had found caught in his clothing when he'd come around. He balanced it. He stared thoughtfully at the ruptors. The yellow ovoid possessed a mass of small bristly spines on its underside by which it had clung to his clothes and, presumably, by which it normally clung to the underside of a geron leaf. It was animal, for he had prised open lids over two small piglike eyes, and had felt the nozzlelike snout that, again presumably, sucked the rich juices from the geron bushes. Dead now, it lay on his hand like a golden prickly hamster.

He turned as the door swung open. Olive Cameron walked in.

"So this is where you're hiding!"

"Hi, sister," he said in his imitation of the way he hoped a normal man would speak. "What's happening out there?"

"Trujillo is having another party. I wondered where you were."

"They like to live it up, don't they, these tycoons of the galaxy?"

She made a face. "With all his money and all his power, what does he really contribute to the galaxy?"

She moved closer to him. This was the first time he had seen her out of uniform. Like most people she wore clothes mainly for functional purposes and when she had no particular purpose she didn't bother. Now the light-colored alice glowed against her skin like a costly pet, as sensual as she was, emphasizing her skin texture. Her breasts were large and rounded, firm, a delight to behold. His impression of her as a dumpy figure he saw to have been a misapprehension born of stiff hospital clothing.

"Oh," he said, as casually as he could. "They contribute quite a bit. I think they're often denigrated without cause."

She reached a hand to his alice and began to stroke

him, meanwhile not ceasing from sensually stroking her own. A rich scent of musk floated from her body.

"He's nice. Sinbad, isn't he? Mine is Florence—for obvious reasons."

Quite clearly, she expected him to stroke her alice. He refrained.

"Appropriate," he said softly, his throat dry. He would have welcomed a woman right now, after all the violence of the previous night; but he felt drained of nervous energy, anxious only to be alone. He had yet to adjust to humanity away from Altimus. There, of course, sex had long been solved as any sort of problem, and the galaxy was almost reaching that beneficent point. But it had not done so yet. He felt his interest stir. She wanted him and he—well, it would be nice and reasonable and comfortable —and, by Astir, he'd finished with being nice and reasonable.

He smiled at **her** and moved away, revealing the glass case and the ruptors.

The hand that had been stroking his alice fell between her breasts. She caught a quick gasp of breath.

"They're horrible!"

"They're dead."

Just what he would have done then he had no clear conception; the door swung again and Eva Vetri walked in.

The contrast between the two women spoke eloquently of variant human origins. Her brown skin glowing, her small bones delicate beneath her velvety skin, her tiny breasts tip tilted, she walked in with a swing, lithely, like a cat. Her alice clung over her shoulder and down her shoulder blades. She smiled mischievously.

"Hello, you two! What are you up to? Kolok Trujillo wants the hero of the hour at the party! We're all waiting! We're going to make up tonight for what was spoilt last night."

"Coming, Eva," said Sister Cameron in a dangerous voice. "I was talking to Mat."

"I'm sure." She waggled her hips. "Dot-Dot was raising merry hell—"

"Oh! Bother!" exclaimed Olive Cameron. She turned the full battery of her eyes on Wade. "Kolok's party should be fun, even though he is—well. . . . I'll see you there, Matthew."

She joined Eva Vetri and the pair went out, an interesting contrast in rear views. Matthew Wade smiled weakly and wiped his forehead.

"Thank your lucky stars you don't have a love life, Sinbad," he symbed.

The response pattern formed a decidedly murky comment.

VII

"The reacton to parasites is fascinatingly various," said Doctor Overbeck, speaking with tremendous energy and authority. "Take *Fascioloides magna*, for example, which persisted only in deer. If the fluke entered the liver of cattle it was killed, whilst if it entered the liver of sheep it killed the sheep. Incidentally, it's not generally known that the fasciolides, including the well-known liver flukes of sheep and cattle, gave the name to all the flukes. The Anglo-Saxons called it Floc. Now in *Dicrocoelium* the cercaria, which has a prehensile tail, enters the cavity of the snail where it becomes covered with mucus and can be swallowed before it leaves the snail or be excreted and eaten by ants—"

"Charming!" The girl, one of Trujillo's party, to whom the doctor of symbiosis was talking so animatedly, lifted a bare, rounded shoulder, gleaming under the lights. She laughed a great deal and liked to let her alice rub against her breasts. She was one of those who singled out the important men in a room and clung, parasitelike, to them alone.

The party had again been held in the headquarters gymnasium and parallel bars and wooden horses, antigrave sinks and calisthenic apparatus had been pushed into the corners so, as Doctor Overbeck had put it, to stop the wallflowers from having corners to crawl into. He liked everyone to join in. Lights blazed down, but not too strongly, so that the dancers could drift along or jimjam in ecstatic rhythm, in a simulactum of private worlds. Streamers and balloons drifted and entwined the dancers. The bar did a brisk trade. Everyone joined the party. Doctor Overbeck wouldn't have liked anyone not to enjoy the party.

Fancy dress was optional.

A fat, bejeweled little man, gesticulating loudly, was talking to Alexander Lokoja, the Kriseman Corporation's chief chemist, whose black face showed only a polite attention and whose massive torso gleamed with health. His alice appeared a dwarfed fur piece around his muscular shoulders.

"We surely get around the galaxy," the fat little man was saying expansively. "Yes, sir, traveling with Kolok sure is some experience."

"You should have come during the harvest here," replied Lokoja with his imperturbable poise. "We use every man and woman then, no matter who."

"What! Me out there in the fields like a hired hand!"

"It's the great day of the year, here, harvest time."

"And the fertility rites, too, huh?"

Lokoja allowed his face to gentle into a sympathetic smile.

"Production of gerontidril is an exact piece of chemical engineering, exacting and dangerous; the harvest is the time for hard work—"

"And then you get to work with your retorts and your distillation apparatus, hey, Alex!" chimed in Eva Vetri. She swirled by in the arms of a young officer from Trujillo's ship, who had difficulty in adjusting his alice to her energetic movements.

"I'm claiming the next dance with you, Eva," replied Lokoja calmly.

Eva Vetri giggled. "Then we're in for the old war dance, hey, Alex!"

She swirled off, a brown sprite, laughing.

"I can imagine her at harvest time." The fat little man licked his lips. Murmuring a polite nothing phrase, Alexander Lokoja moved away.

The party so far remained a sedate affair, not yet having generated enough steam for an orgy, although some of the younger personnel of the base and from Trujillo's entourage were mutually teaching one another some of the newer and more exotic pastimes culled from a galaxy of pleasure. Matthew Wade, for reasons he didn't bother to analyze, drifted around the gym on his perambulating course away from that brightly youthful sink.

By this time he had reached an inescapable conclusion. Despite his renunciation of the exalted status of a coord of Altimus, he nevertheless remained a coord. Although he had switched off those extra circuits in his brain, he retained enough of the elan vital of the coord born to want to know and experience his environment in toto. No other way of life had ever seemed worthwhile to him. So he knew, with a whimsical little self-mockery, that he would snoop and probe and pry until he had come up with the answers to the problems that, self-evidently, were troubling the authorities on this Kriseman Corporation Headquarters base on Ashramdrego.

As far as he knew the culture of the geron bushes proceeded satisfactorily. Alexander Lokoja, after the harvest, would process the crop into gerontidril. That secret process served as the foundation stone of Kriseman's fortunes on this world. That was why everyone was here.

Even the problem of the ruptors was solvable. Luis Perceau, there, scowling over his drink by the bar, knew one answer.

Tom Martin, still shaky, but coming up with a bright smile for all the pretty young things gyrating away on the dance floor, now, might share a different viewpoint; but between them Ashramdrego's military force would handle the ruptors.

Sergeant Goudsmit, having been duly and solemnly buried, was by mutual consent not allowed to interfere with the continued desire for enjoyment of the living.

"You were damn lucky, Tom," Perceau took another drink, moodily. "As for the delay in rescuing you—Sergeant Trudeau's relieving an eepee on latrine duty."

"Sar'nt Goudsmit only sent in a request for reinforcements. You didn't know we were in trouble."

"Knocking down ruptors is one of the reasons we're here, we few military men, Tom. All we are, really, that side of our work, is glorified pest controllers—"

"Um."

"Still and all, by Astir, you were lucky. Much longer out there without an alice and your blood would have reverted to normal terrestrial hemoglobin-based blood and then—"

"Don't—"

"I'm going to press Sternmire damned hard to use hormones." Perceau's ugly face glowered balefully over his glass. "Goddamit, Tom! It's one thing when the crop is ruined, it's another when a man of my command gets killed!"

So that, surmised Matthew Wade, walking past, was what rankled with Luis Perceau. The military mind, like any other phenomenon of mankind in the galaxy, could be melded into the life equations by a coord; but that did not stop Wade from feeling a peculiarly human abhorrence for the man himself, an almost irrational drawing back from a fellow human being.

The young D.D.O. saw him and smiled.

"Hallo, Mat. Drinking?"

"A cautious, mild but interesting wine." He essayed a little in joke. "If you'll kindly step back a pace, I'll bow three times."

"How's that?" asked Perceau.

Martin's smile did not widen. "Oh, Mat here is a

fellow Molièreist. Still and all, I'm beginning to wonder. Those ruptors made me think—"

"Oh," said Wade. His smile, a tentative offering, faded.

Hans Kremer, the botanist, tall and abrupt, pushed past with an apology, balancing four glasses. "Don't talk to me about ruptors," he said, plonking the glasses down. His alice opened an eye, surveyed the scene and closed up shop. "I almost wish geron bushes didn't naturally grow in rows. At least that'd give those damned destructive pests a harder time."

"Do they?" asked Wade. "I mean, naturally in rows?"

"Yes. They have a mutual root system. We just trim the side stems, a sort of strawberry runner effect."

Wade took the yellow ovoid from his pocket and held it out. "What's this?"

Kremer bent to peer. Martin and Perceau badgered the barrobot for fresh drinks.

"Oh, that's a symbiont on the leaves. We thought they were a pest at first; but a few tests showed that they derived nourishment from the juices and their half of the bargain was to fix nitrogen. They have a mass of bacteria—you know, the leguminous plant root system all over again."

Wade knew.

"In massive form, of course. You can't expect alien botany to follow terrestrial norms all the time. We call them plomps. How'd you come by it?"

Wade explained. "They seem rather juicy in themselves."

"We lost Pankowski, the biologist, in the, ah, troubles. We've done nothing like enough research on

Drego. So far we don't know the life cycle of the plomps—"

"Let alone the squoodles—"

"Huh? Oh, the alices. Yes, unfortunately. But we're working on it. As you can imagine, the director wants everything concentrated on geron production. Everything."

The botanist took his filled glasses and wandered off, a tall figure, his alice like a ruff of brown fur.

Questions without answers were anathema to Wade. He took himself away from the bar, with a filled glass, to probe further. Maybe, as the old saying had it, he ought to think up the right answers, first, before the questions. The taped music died as the cassette ran out and a robot opened his chest and began to reload. Kriseman used robots sparingly. With electroplasms so much more easily available —although the electroplasm master had died in the troubles—the humans equipped with alices vastly more efficient at the intricate cerebral and decision-making tasks required here, the Kriseman Corporation got along very well. As the music swelled out again, Doctor Marian Anstee, laughing and flushed, spun out of the crowd and cannoned into Wade.

For a fleeting moment he thought her action deliberate, then he saw the handsome and uniform-wearing ship's captain, flaunting his insignia, plunge after her, brushing aside a dancing chem lad operator and a radar mech. Marian Anstee clung for a moment to Wade, laughing and breathless.

He put an arm around her waist to support her. She wore a diaphanous costume of flame nylon, with rows of tiny gems, and her golden hair had been caught up into an extravagant topknot overloaded with diamonds. He wondered why she thought it necessary to vulgarize the perfect.

Even her alice had a pearl collar.

"Oh, Mr. Wade. Thank you."

She straightened up and he had to let his hand drop away from the firm warm tautness of her waist.

"C'mon, Marian! The dance is starting again!"

"Oh, Guy! I'm all out of breath!"

Wade felt a savage satisfaction that his circuits were switched off so that he could luxuriate in the aberrant atavism of hating the handsome captain on sight.

Swaggering, gilded, bearded, with flared nostrils and sensuous lips, the captain caught Marian Anstee's arm and began to draw her back into the throng.

"You're enjoying this, Marian. I know you are. C'mon!"

She threw Wade a comical look.

"I was just going to ask Mr. Wade—"

"Forget the creep! *I'm* dancing with you—"

The captain's flamboyant and unintentionally juvenile golden earring danced above his alice. Every now and then the alice burped and shifted around, only to be carelessly and ungently shoved back by the captain's broad competent hand.

"If Doctor Anstee doesn't wish to dance any more," began Wade. He knew this situation from theory and knew the various theoretical solutions. A deep dark welling of delight that horrified him even as he soaked in its therapeutic potential suggested he would favor the solution that called for him to poke this guy in the jaw.

"Keep out of this, creep. Marian's dancing with me."

Her comical look remained, frozen in a stasis of irresolution. To Wade, she still looked lovely, despite her expression, despite her ridiculous costume.

"What were you going to ask me, Doctor Anstee?"

"That doesn't matter now." The captain hauled on Marian's arm as though hauling in a tarpon. "Come to me, baby. Let's dance. I've got plans, baby, big plans—"

Wade's disgust must have shown in his face, for Marian broke her frozen stasis to smile, a little forlornly, and then she was dragged off into the hurlyburly of the dance.

A massive black form and a slight brown sprite pirouetted past.

"A wonderful doctor of symbiosis," rumbled Alexander Lokoja, "but a weak-willed woman in every other sphere."

"My foot!" shrilled Eva Vetri. "Keep your mind on dancing, Alex, you lecherous old cannibal!"

"And I shall not need any spice on you, my spitfire!"

Relieved, Wade chuckled, and moved away. He'd see Marian Anstee again. Trujillo's supercilious ship captain wouldn't be staying too long on planet, thanks be.

Still and all, he mused, aiming himself for an alcove between the trampoline and suspension rings where Silas Sternmire and Kolok Trujillo stood talking, how did he explain, in view of her obvious limitations, his absorbing interest in Marian Anstee? Surely not merely a perfect body? Not really, surely, not at his age. Then again, at any age, come to think of it. He chuckled, amused.

A woman, who would best be described as a

magnificent animal, lounged on the trampoline. Her kohled eyes regarded Trujillo with a remote, ready look. Her body, sheathed in purple nylon, gleamed like white fire through the material. Her sumptuousness of curves could shatter a male ego. Two or three young men, hangers-on in Trujillo's retinue, adored her in a worshipping cluster. To Wade, thinking of Marian Anstee, she seemed quite a nice looking gal.

Trujillo, as usual, monopolized the conversation, pausing only, in his tycoonish way, for answers that served as a counterpoint to his argument.

He broke off as Wade approached, saying: ". . . Godforsaken planets at all, Silas, without the damn alices into the bargain." He grunted at Sternmire harrumphed.

"Here comes the hero now, Kolok. This is Mr. Wade."

Trujillo looked Wade up and down with the habitual air of a man sizing up an opponent, without insult and yet flagrantly insulting all the same. Wade smiled.

"Wade, this is Mr. Trujillo. You've heard of him, of course."

"Of little else since he arrived. I hope you're enjoying yourself on Ashramdrego, Mr. Trujillo."

"Seems you saved a soldier's life by quick thinking, Wade. Although I can't go along one hundred percent with this natural symbiosis life support system. If you'd just shoved up a dome down here, used spacesuits and planetary crawlers or fliers outside—the damn geron bushes have to grow in their own atmosphere but you don't have to live in it, surely."

73

Sternmire's doughy features took on their indulgent look. "But you have a symb-socket fixed, Kolok. Everyone who travels the galaxy in anything other than a simple terrestrial type planet hopping does. It makes sense."

Trujillo's thick features with the pendulous cheeks and rattrap mouth slipped into a laugh. His tiny eyes, pouched and beady, betrayed jollity. A thick built man, with strong imperious gestures, he had ruled Trujillo Enterprises Corporation for fifty years and, with the help of gerontidril, would go on doing so for another four hundred fifty or more.

"I know you're right, Silas. It does make sense. But I grew up with the concept of man in space as living in oxygen-helium or oxygen-nitrogen domes, wearing suits, dependent on his air cylinders—"

"That's all old-fashioned now, Mr. Trujillo, in places where a symbiote is to be found."

"Don't interrupt me, Wade, please." Trujillo didn't glower and his voice remained boredly steady.

"Really, Wade!" reprimanded Sternmire.

The shock to Wade was that he had forgotten for that instant, talking to a man like Trujillo, that he was no longer a coord of Altimus.

"I assumed by your voice inflection that you had finished," he contented himself with saying.

"I hadn't. And if what I was saying is so old-fashioned, it's at least the way men first ventured into space. I built an empire like that."

Wade killed his desire to say: "Finished?" Instead he said: "But with doctors of symbiosis at your beck and call you can operate your profitable businesses on world that would have presented tremendous problems with merely mechanical life support systems."

"I do run, and I run at a profit. I've got a million people working for me, Wade, and don't you forget it. I can make or break a man. Even Kriseman has respect for me."

Wade had to get out of this conversation somehow. He turned to Sternmire, and said: "I wanted to speak to you about—about that game of marbles."

"Marbles!" huffed Trujillo. "What the hell are you up to, Wade? By Astir, you'd better clear off before you say something you'll be sorry for!"

"Yes, Wade, you'd better cut along!" Sternmire's squashy face expressed the outrage of a man encountering not only T. S. Eliot and W. H. Auden but also Verlaine.

Without another word, Wade turned to leave.

The exotic woman rose from the trampoline, felinelike, gracefully, letting the trampoline do the work, landing softly before Wade. She smiled and her lipstick clung momentarily to her lips, running like a scarlet magne fastener from center to corners.

"I'd like to dance, Mr. Wade."

"Sure, Cleo, you do that," said Trujillo.

Wade saw, clearly, that he had a thing going at the moment with this woman and had no wish to upset the balance he must have been at pains to construct over the trip to Drego. He nodded curtly and held out his arms.

She floated into him. Her purple cat suit flowed along her body like smoke. She moved into him. They danced out onto the floor, and he felt the heat of her body bore into him, churning up the secret places inside, paining in his loins.

She tilted her dark head up.

"You don't dance very well, Mr. Wade."

What should he say to that?

"Lack of practice," he mumbled.

She danced barefoot. Her white body was bare, too, beneath the smoky veil of the purple cat suit. Stunningly bereft of any jewelry, she had twined a priceless platinum and bellachrontis bracelet around her alice.

After his first male and adolescent reaction to her, Wade was not enjoying this dance. They gyrated among the others, hearing the laughter and shrill talk, catching wafting scents and perfumes, brushing aside trailing streamers and, with the first giggle gas balloons of the evening, avoiding their insidious fumes.

An eepee waiter scurried by with a silver tray balanced on his cranial box. The girl, Cleo, snatched a dribbling handful of candies, began idly to feed her alice as they danced. She moved her body against Wade. He began to feel the need for air.

Then a pattern formed in his mind, and Sinbad made unmistakably known his own desire for eggs, and, failing those, for candies. As the eepee galloped back, Wade obliged his alice.

"I wouldn't upset Kolok, if I was you."

"It was purely unintentional."

"He's a very big man."

"I'm sure."

"Why don't you like me?"

"Why what? I like you."

"Then hold me as though you did. I'm not going to bite you."

"But Trujillo might."

She pouted and chuckled and squeezed his back.

"He's frightened he's going to lose me. Captain Kirkus's beard gives him nightmares."

Wade laughed.

"You must have real fun on your trips in space."

"You could call it that. I know what I want, and nothing in this man's galaxy is going to stop me getting it."

Holding her like this, he could clearly see the point of junction at the base of her neck where her arterial blood system joined with that of her alice. Normally, an alice lay so that he covered the junction. Now, in her movements, Cleo had moved the alice aside. Wade watched fascinated as the thick umbilical cord pulsed with blood. Her symb-socket, he saw, was as new as his own.

A hand touched Wade's arm.

A smart young lieutenant in uniform stood politely waiting.

"I'm cutting in," he said perfunctorily, and took Cleo's wrist, moving Wade aside.

"Oh, Basil! I suppose the big chief sent you. He gets so jealous," she pouted back at Wade. With a dazzling smile she whirled away, the spaceship lieutenant nuzzling himself up in this brief moment of glorious contact before he delivered her safe and sound back to the trampoline.

Wade gave a grimace and turned and was bowled into by a dancing couple. He almost fell, righted himself by a quick snapping movement of body coordination. Now if only they'd been dancing a normal out-and-swing-in dance instead of these modern resurrected twentieth century body contact dances, he'd have been all right—

"Out of the way, oaf!"

The captain glowered at him, swinging Marian Anstee by. She had her eyes closed. Her body more sagged against the spaceman than danced of its own volition.

Before Wade could say anything they had swept on into the dancing press.

He walked, dodging dancers, to the bar.

The military had decamped.

The party upped a gear, swung into a wilder rhythm. The giggle gas balloons were partly responsible. But a feeling of orgy began to create its own abandonment of censorship. At one time Matthew Wade had quite enjoyed a good swinging orgy and he could still welcome the diversion and catharsis an orgy could provide; but right now he suffered a revulsion in his mood. The omens, if you wished, were not propitious.

He had a couple more drinks of the bland wine and then decided to call it a night.

The keen incisive voice was saying: ". . . organisms are parasitic only sometimes in their development. Like the monstrilloida which are free swimming as adults and parasitic as larvae. And, too, *Monstrilla heligolandica* is a parasite of gastropods, and they in their turn are parasitic on lamellibranchs." Doctor Overbeck's obsession with his work dominated the fluttering eye flirtings of his half-naked girl from Trujillo's ship.

"It all sounds disgusting to me," she giggled, half nauseated, Wade saw.

"It is strange how the wonderful workings of parasitism can arouse infantile feelings of fear and disgust."

Wade walked on. Doctors of symbiosis must have a tough time of it finding something smart and light to talk about in parasitology to their birds.

Somebody else shared similar if more forcibly expressed sentiments about Doctor Overbeck. As Wade walked out of the gym and into the soft breathing darkness of the Dregoan night he heard a voice raised raucously.

". . . Overbeck! He's nothing but a confounded cocksure cee-dot-dot-tee of a doctor! I'd like to see him perform a simple tonsillectomy! Or diagnose the most common complaints the poor old ess-dot-dee of a G.P. has to handle every day of the eff-dot-dot-gee week!"

"Now, doctor! That's no way to talk about a fellow practitioner!" Sister Olive Cameron, invisible in the night. "Now just let me take you—"

"Fellow practitioner my aye-dot-dot-ee!"

Wade chuckled, at a bound regaining his good spirits. He still wouldn't duck back into the consummation of the coming orgy; but he refrained now for different reasons from those that had driven him out of the gym.

The two voices, the rumble of dot-dots and the soothing syrupy professional balm, receded.

Wade glanced up. Poisonous gases swathed the planet heavily now and the stars remained invisible. From his window high on the topmost peak of Altimus the stars had shone down bright and near and comradely.

Standing in the shadows like that—how often had he stood in the shadows since fleeing from Altimus —he saw Captain Kirkus and Marian Anstee leave the gym.

"No, really," Marian was saying. She walked as though drugged, her head rolling so that her cheek brushed her alice.

"Oh, come on, baby! We're all in the traveler's rest house Kriseman provided. It's not the Ritz, baby; but my room is cozy and nice and private. . . . C'mon!"

At first amusement made Wade wonder what sort of orgy it was thumping away in there among the lights and the music if these two had to opt out for their own purposes. He had no lien on Marian Anstee and she could do exactly as she wanted. She did know he existed, for apart from anything else she had given him Sinbad; but to her he was merely another name and number on her operations timetable. That he felt this attraction to her had already caused him severe misgivings about his whole motivations in discarding those extra circuits in his brain.

The captain was really dragging Marian now, one arm pressing familiarly around her waist. Her feet slid on the slabs of the walk. She tried to lift her head.

"I don't think—no, really, I don't want to—"

"But you know you like it! And it's not far, in the next block. . . ." His hot whisper reached Wade and his amusement began to sour.

Silhouetted in the lights, the two of them—the gallant captain and the female doctor of symbiosis —formed a clear enough picture. Disliking what he was getting himself into, unhappy about the whole thing, Wade started to take a belligerent step forward.

Taking him completely by surprise, a high angry

voice burst out behind him and the sound of running and staggering feet on the stone slabs sent him
back to his friendly shadows.

"Hey!" A hiccup, whether from alice or man he
couldn't say. "What the atich-dot-dot-ell's going
on! Marian, are you all right?"

Another voice, the syrup congealed.

"Doctor! Come back this instant!"

"Get eff-dot-dot-dee, you old killjoy! He's after
our Marian, the confounded bee-dot-dot-dee!"

Captain Kirkus looked up snappishly, his face ugly.
His eyes went mean. In the reflected light he looked
like a cheap one-night stand imitation of Mephis-
topheles. He put out a fist and struck Doc Hedges
on the nose. The doc spilt over backward, fell with
a string of dot-dots spattering the night air. Olive
Cameron screamed.

Marian Anstee let rip a tiny scream and sagged
back.

Reluctantly, feeling a mountebank, Matthew Wade
at last stepped out of the shadows into the light.

VIII

"So it's the hick hero!"

Nothing about the petty scene excited Wade.
Olive Cameron knelt by Doc Hedges, mopping at his
bleeding nose, while old Dot-Dot exploded in a
Morse code of curses.

"I don't believe Marian Anstee knows quite what
she's doing," Wade said carefully, and then at once
saw the enormity of such a statement. But he had
made it; now he'd have to stick by it.

"Get lost, sonny! I know what I'm doing. C'mon, Marian, baby, it's not far, and then—"

"I'm not—no, really—I feel woozy—"

She was not drunk. Wade saw alert now, nor, he felt reasonably sure, was she drugged. The poor girl was just dead tired and careless of what was going on. Maybe she'd caught a fringe whiff of a giggle gas balloon and the effect had aborted, as it sometimes did. She was in no mood for romantic bed; she needed a bed just to sleep in.

"You'd better let Doctor Anstee go to her room."

The space captain tried to push past. "She's going where I'm taking her, creep. By Astir, get out of my sight!"

Stiff lipped now, Wade spoke curtly. "I'm afraid I can't allow that. Doctor Anstee is in no condition—"

He was cut off by Kirkus enraged bellow, the voice of a man habituated to instant obedience.

"Keep out of my way, flatlander! By Astir, you'll rue the day the T.S.C. probe ever picked up Ashramdrego and thus provided a stage for you to meet me!" He swung a hard and heavy punch at Wade.

Expecting to be struck, as Dot-Dot Hedges had been struck, Wade was able to skip aside. Since the days when he had cheerfully brawled with his kid companions he had scarcely been involved in a fist fight, save that one time on Takkarnia. He had a moment for introspective disbelief and wonderment at his own atavistic hunger for what was to come. Then he found himself involved in the whirlwind.

Hampered as he was by the limp but protesting form of Marian Anstee, Captain Kirkus's blow fell short, and his next attempt could be blocked by Wade's left forearm. Wade struck out.

His sensations poured in in a chaotic bedlam. He felt the blow drive home, the gristle of beard and the jarring shock of bone. He struck again, harder, clumsily, felt the return blow graze along his cheek, stinging him, and then, with a final excess of fury, sublimely contemptible, he smashed his closed fist down across the captain's nose.

He caught Marian as she stumbled and fell.

Kirkus, rousing himself, tried to kick Wade's ankles from under him. Surprising himself, Wade kicked back. The captain dropped limp.

"Oh!" said Marian, drowsily.

"Bed for you," said Wade. He felt as though the euphoria possessing him as he'd left the gym had exploded in pancolor and lights. He cradled the girl's body, then lifted her, got a hand under her knees, and, without looking back at Kirkus, took her off.

Olive Cameron looked up with a long intense glance.

"I'd better come along and help," she said swiftly. "Doctor Anstee's probably—"

"Good idea," Wade said, simon pure. Then, diabolically, he added: "What about Doc Hedges?"

"Oh—" Olive Cameron looked down. Her handkerchief tissues were now a wadded bloodied splodge. "I'll—"

"Get me to the bee-dot-dot-wye surgery, Olive!"

Chuckling, Wade made off into the darkness, holding warm softness in his hands. He halted. A frown chased across his face. He recalled the dust, the geron leaves, his own suspicion. At once he swung back and, still holding Marian, bent above Kirkus. The man bubbled through mashed lips. His nose bled. But he was conscious and about to try to stand up. Relieved, Wade left him and took Doctor Marian Anstee to her room.

Small, neat, lightly perfumed, the room revealed only facets of her personality he would have expected. He put her on the bed and, working with calmness and no undue haste or tardiness, he undressed her, washed her, tucked her in and then withdrew, turning off the light.

His head still in the opening, he heard her stir, a silken rustle of bedclothes.

"Mr. Wade? Don't go."

He heard her slither out of bed. The bedside lamp went on.

A single enormous thump pounded his heart.

She stood there, the sheets half draped about her, smiling uncertainly at him. He went back in slowly.

"Look, thank you for—for whatever it is you did. I remember that awful captain man, and then—I feel better now, but still tired."

"Get," he swallowed and started over. "Get some rest."

He hoped—he admitted it without shame—he hoped she would smile and negate that order with a soft command he could not resist.

She did smile. She did negate his command. But she said: "Look, I ought to get down to the lab. I've an experiment running and I must—it went out of my head, what with the party and that space captain. I'll have to get dressed and get down there right away."

He had to laugh. Here he had been expecting you-know-what, and she had to attend to a laboratory experiment.

Sure he had to laugh.

They walked quickly through the breathing night, their alices stirring and hiccuping around their necks, mocking them for so much activity so late. Drego's gravity of point nine five of Earth normal made it no burden to carry an alice around; but the alices liked to sleep, too, so Sinbad symbed a mock-protest pattern.

The laboratory, although outwardly constructed of local Drego wood and stone, inside contained a modern plastic and glass complex of machinelike precision. Fluorescents lit up as they entered. Whiteness, sterility, glass cages, tubing, massive electrical energy sources, all surrounded them with the intestinal fabrication of practicing symbiotic medicine.

Marian crossed to a desk set against a wall and, opening a drawer, quickly swallowed a pick-up pill. She smiled a little weakly and brushed a hand through her hair, at first passing six inches too high to cover the pile of golden diamond-studded hair Wade had let down.

"Oh—you"

At once he pointed to a large glass case, isolated against the end wall, softly lit.

"What's that?"

She glanced once, then walked in the opposite direction.

"An orbovtia. We don't see many now although when Doctor Overbeck first landed they thronged the virgin forests where we planted the geron bushes."

Decidedly, the orbovita should have repelled a

human, with its dangling clump of tendrils over eight feel long, its lumpish body with tiny features arranged in a facsimile of a cocker spaniel's face, and the drooping flaccid folds of a huge sac depending to one side like a collapsed marquee. The eyes were closed. The mouth had been forced open and Wade saw the ruminant teeth, the blackened areas which should have been healthy red.

"What's—" he began.

Marian was bending over a lab bench and, without turning, she said: "That sac swells up in life. The things float about, rather than the Portuguese Man-of-war in Earth's seas."

"In the atmosphere? Hydrogen?"

"As soon as an orbovita dies the sac deflates. So far we haven't had time to investigate thoroughly." She clucked and adjusted an instrument, absorbed. "We've been concentrating entirely on the alices and the geron bushes."

"Seems to me there hasn't been time for a whole lot of basic research on Drego."

She looked up quickly as Wade joined her, her face flushed. She brushed a strand of golden hair from her forehead. "Kriseman knows what it's doing, Mr. Wade. Although, sometimes, I wonder what we're all here for, what it's all about. . . ."

"The answers to that one don't necessarily depend on an I.Q. Rather on a Z.F.L.Q."

Twin arrows furrowed her brows. "Z.F.L.Q?"

He chuckled gently. "It's a measurement we used on—well, never mind that. A Zest For Living Quotient. When you have a goal and go all out for it. When you're living at the top of your form. Then you see the answers and you ferret out the questions."

Her smile responded to him. "I like that."

"What's the experiment?"

Her smile vanished. He caught an intangible feel of guilt, of small-girl mischief, of confusion.

"I don't believe you'd really understand, Mr. Wade. It's symbiotic blood typing."

"I know who first sorted out the different blood types. Doctor Karl Landsteiner, born in 1868 in Baden, Austria. He found the A and B substances and he called blood without them O, for naught, so—"

"—so later on people misread that O and called it the better O, for O blood. Well, Mr. Wade, you surprise me."

"Do the alices here have compatible blood, or do you have to modify it?"

"And now you disappoint me! That's a silly question."

He smiled deprecatingly. "Right answer, wrong question."

A chirrup sound from a glass case into which thick air hoses pumped, purring in the general quiet. Inside the case four or five chimpanzees began to stir, disturbed by the light. None wore an alice.

"We use them. They're pets and we don't hurt them. That case has a normal terrestrial atmosphere."

"So it's their prison, then?"

She winced. "Prison. I hate the word. They all have symb-sockets. I know about prisons, and I'd sever every iron bar in the whole galaxy, if I could."

"That way a gaggle of undesirables might be let loose."

She returned to her work. Wade watched. They

spoke desultorily, but gradually Wade built up a freer mood between them, a feeling of comradeship heightened by the late hour, the apartness of the laboratory, the pool of light in which they stood.

Absorbed, she kept her mind on her work; but Wade turned her onto talking about herself. "Oh, yes, Mr. Wade. I was born into a wealthy family. On Earth. I went to one of the best schools Earthside, Bedgebury. The Pinetum created an interest in botany. Then there was Oxford. After that medicine. Parasitology led me on to symbiosis. I thought the galaxy needed dedicated doctors of symbiosis."

"You're right. The galaxy does."

She put down the hypospray and her hands shook. "I'm so unsure. I feel like a traitor."

She leaned against the lab bench for support. Her face had lost its color. Evidently, the pick-up pill needed a pick up itself.

"Would you like to tell me about it, Doctor Anstee?"

She licked her lips. Something in this girl needed support, needed to find a sounding board with sympathy.

"I suppose, you'd better call me Marian."

"Mat."

"I've been going out of my mind, lately. After the troubles—it was horrible, and there's no one to turn to."

Shrewdly, feeling less than a man as he made the suggestion, Wade said: "You could have discussed the problem with Doc Hedges."

She grimaced. "Dot-Dot is a fine doctor but he's an M.D. Doctor Overbeck and I have gone way beyond that."

Wade took a breath. He had to prod her now. "Yet Dot-Dot says the alices are dangerous."

She started.

"He's right! They're deadly!"

She swung away from the bench. Her hands shook. Her face showed strain and despair. "But why should I talk about it to you? You don't understand. Who are you, anyway?"

"First of all, I'm a friend. And you've got to talk to somebody or you'll blow up. And I'd guess Dot-Dot, for all that he's a fine doctor with an expensive bedside manner, is regarded as a buffoon. People don't take notice of him, because he's prejudiced their minds against him."

"I—yes, that's right."

"How are the alices deadly?"

She did not reply.

He took her arm, conscious of her flesh beneath his fingers, walked her across to a bench, sat her down and sat beside her. He put an arm around her waist.

"Now, Marian. Look at this thing logically. You're a doctor of symbiosis—"

"I'm young! Untried. How do I know what's right."

"In parallel I'd like to know why Kriseman has two symbiotists down here. Surely one would be enough to process the personnel?"

"Doctor Overbeck, he's a great man, Mat, truly a wonderful person. He worked with Doctor Arliss for a few years, just before Arliss died."

"Doctor Arliss, when he pioneered and put through the whole symbiotic idea, earned the gratitude of the entire galaxy. Any man who worked with him must have been touched with his greatness. I don't know Doctor Overbeck, as yet; but you haven't answered my question. No," he put a finger to his lips. "You don't have to. That's a question for which I've already seen the answer, seen it in action. The alices take off. They decamp. And that's what happened in the troubles."

"Yes," she whispered. "It was horrible. Men and women suddenly bereft of their life support systems on a planet so hostile to our life, so vicious and cruel, so—"

"All right, all right."

But he spoke gently.

"We tried to strap them on, to hold them fixed to their symbiont; but they just withdrew their cord and their host died, and we found them out in the fields—it was horrible!"

A flashing moment of pain occurred to Wade as he wondered if any of these dark meanings were seeping over to Sinbad, being symbed willy-nilly to his alice. He hoped fervently that they were not.

"So there's a problem," he said flatly. "What is Doctor Overbeck doing about it?"

She shook her head helplessly. "What can he do, Mat? He came in with the first Kriseman team. They found the squoodles seeming absolutely perfect for symbionts. There are many life forms on Drego, the planet is rich in life, although we've found no traces of highly intelligent life. In fact, the squoodles responded to our symb patterns beautifully. And there they were, on our doorstep. Doctor Overbeck did what anyone would have done."

"He chose them for alices. And they work, or else we'd be sitting here in air suits or under a dome wondering when it would puncture, like they cower on airless worlds. Yes. It fits. But then you come along, asked for by Doctor Overbeck."

"Yes. I was so happy and excited."

"And you walk right slap into the middle of a problem you feel you can't handle. That the symbiotist who has the biggest reputation in the galaxy right now can't be wrong, and yet. . . ."

"And yet I'm sure he is, Mat! But Doctor Overbeck wrong and refusing to listen, and me—what can I do?"

"Well—" He didn't like this. "For one thing—"

"You see, Mat, I love him. I've never loved anyone like this before. He's so—so—and I believe he's wrong, and I love him and we're all going to be killed!"

IX

BROTHER STANLEY WAS DEAD. He'd been gunned down by a trigger-happy tipstaff from Altimus. Now even the oozing puddle of slime that was all that remained of him would have dissipated, run down the drain.

The horror of that painted a scarlet mask of forgetfulness over Matthew Wade's actions. He came back to a semblance of normalcy spacing into Samia; and he recalled his reasons for seeking passage to the planet of the Demons. Here, for a price and at a cost of surrending a little of one's own ego, a Samian camouflage cloak could be obtained. A deep, soul-wrenching hunger for anonymity possessed Wade. He wanted to be able to draw his cloak about him and blend with the landscape and be overlooked.

As a superlative computer man and able to demonstrate that aptitude, he had no difficulty in finding gainful occupation. Among the land of the Giants terrestrial-sized people had built up a lively culture of their own, freed from the rat runs and pest holes of their former lives behind the wainscoting and in the walls of the Demons' houses. Wade bought his cloak, submitting to the minor operation that joined Lon Chaney's tendrils to his own central nervous system. Here, in a rude but nonetheless extraordinary effective fashion was an early example of symbiosis between different planetary species.

He grew to love Lon Chaney. The cape's sixteen legs clung around his body, artfully shifting as he moved, giving him cover and concealment. He spaced out from the planet of the Demons no happier but infinitely more at ease.

His experiment with poor doomed Brother Stanley of trying to live on a brawling frontier world had not succeeded. He considered then rejected the idea of traveling to Solterra. One day, he promised himself, he would visit Earth as a non coord; but he could not face the home of mankind now, in his present frame of mind. So he settled for Takkarnia, one of the planets of the Tak system, those ancient enemies of Solterra along with Shurilala in the evil TEST wars. Those days lay in the distant past, even before Strathan, the genius of comic vision, had taken up the direct line of comic genius from Molière and Plautus. Another strange echo from the future reverberated in the coming meeting with Tom Martin on as yet unheard of Ashramdrego. . . .

After the fracas on Takkarnia he had shifted only once more, to a job on the hostile planet called Catspaw. Left alone by the Solterran Construction Service as unearthlike, it had been found to contain minerals and chemicals that made a bonus sideline in mining to the main chore of collecting monocerate, and that, as schoolchildren learned, was as rare as a snowflake on Sungard VI.

Matthew Wade spaced down in a company ship to Catspaw.

In the terrestrial dome he waited in the line for the unsocketed. Men and women around him talked and laughed and shuffled nervously forward. This planet was being run by the Liang-Peng Corporation and their doctor of symbiosis had trained briefly under Doctor Arliss himself.

In line ahead of Wade a pair of brothers talked with bright toughness. The elder, a thick-necked confident fellow with a symb-socket already surgically implanted, joshed his younger brother.

"There's nothing to it, Fered. Just nothing at all."

"Mother did say—"

"I know! D'you think I'd space all the way home to fix my kid brother up with a swell job if I didn't know what I was talking about?"

"Gee, Dav, I guess I'm excited! I mean, out in space and all, and me right from college. And already I'm having a symb-socket fixed."

"Like I was telling you, last contract I served we was on this planet, see, where they had damn great mammoths as alices! Man, did we ride proud!"

"I hear they've a copepod magna here, whatever that is."

"I've heard tell it's a nauplius; but, gee, Fered, it don't matter what alice the docs decide on. They know what they're doin', for Astir's sake!"

Wade said, "The word copepod comes from the Greek: *kope* for oar, and *pous* for foot, or leg."

"Hark at the prof!"

A chorus of pained remarks broke out in the waiting line. Wade smiled. They'd already tagged him for his camouflage cloak.

"I was just going to say that the first stages of a copepod are called a nauplius. On Earth the animals are very small, and they grow by adding segments to the larva. Usually they have sixteen segments and five pairs of feet."

"So long as I get a free ride on one pair of feet, I won't mind!"

The line moved up. These men with their toughly arrogant galactic laboring attitude—all men capable of handling electronic machinery, eepee decision making, statistical doctrines—formed a glittering society among the stars. No wonder younger brothers like Fered worshiped their older, space-hardened brothers like Dav.

The symbiosis theater struck a single chord of teror in Wade. Then he had cussed himself for an idiot and entered to lie on the operating table indicated. The doctor smiled mechanically and initiated proceedings by nodding to the anesthetist who popped his hypospray against Wade's bare arm.

When he came around he sat up without a trace of dizziness. He felt his neck as the doctor waited for the next patient. Under his fingers he could feel the smooth round annulus of the socket, his own skin grafted over the circular junction. A flap of skin lay, a little wrinkled, to one side.

"The flap will be used to cover the socket when you're not using your alice," a nurse said, leading him to the exit door. Another patient lay on the operating table. "It'll grow more pliable in a couple of days. Should you feel any irritation at all—any at all, mind—report back here. That's all there is to it. Indoctrination will be in the main hall at fifteen hundred hours."

A laughing crowd of newly inducted symb-socketeers crowded outside, drinking coffee, waiting for the indoctrination session. They all took it in their various strides. Wade touched his own socket. He couldn't feel it there as an excrescence on his own body. It was just a new part of him, only to be noticed when it failed. You were never conscious of your own body when it ran perfectly; only sickness made you conscious of any part.

The indoctrination was brief.

The doctor of symbiosis—a mild, bored little man whose name, Wade thought, was Fanxter or Frankster—had the greatest claim to fame in that he had studied with Doctor Arliss. He called for quiet, standing at the end of the room. He peered at the new inductees.

He began: "You're here to work for the Liang-Peng Corporation collecting monocerate, mining, running various plants. The Corporation could have handled this operation in the old traditional way on a hostile nonterrestrial planet by using air domes, air-filled crawlers, air suits. Then, I'm sure, you'd all have felt the usual desire to have an extra supply of air cylinders handy—"

One or two of the men laughed.

"There are cutting acids out there in some of the oceans you're going to work. You'd have been exchanging armored suits every week. You wouldn't have been able to see very well except by continually using radar or thermoprobes and infrareds. On Catspaw all these functions are carried out by your symbiont."

A screen at his back lit up. Men and woman checked automatic gasps. Pictured on the screen an animal gazed out, many segmented, possessing many pairs of oarlike feet. It moved freely.

"A copepod magna. On Earth they are often parasitic during the larval stages and free swimming when adults. Caligoida are parasitic and can leave their host—well, these animals are so small on Earth; but here, with a different evolutionary environment —you'll be carried by your alice like a man on horseback."

"Suits me," said Fered, daring. Dav glared.

"Symbiosis is a very wonderful thing and a very fragile thing. Why did birds perch on the backs of cattle and sheep or creep about in the formidable jaws of crocodiles? Why did fish shelter under *Physalia?* Why do caterpillars of the large blue butterfly, *Maculinea arion,* hunch themselves up and ask to be carried by ants to their nest? Although, I grant, this has been called more commensalism, feeding together, than symbiosis. The lichens, which are really threads of a fungus and the green cells of algae, give an answer—"

One or two of the inductees leaned back, concealing yawns. They knew all this already. But Wade felt interest in watching the reactions of the others, which mostly consisted of trying to keep their bottom jaws from falling.

"The fungus is deficient in chlorophyll but takes carbohydrates from the alga which has chlorophyll and processes them from the carbon dioxide by photosynthesis. The fungus completes its side of the bargain by providing nutrient rich salt water. Most people know that lichens are really a fungus and an alga; few understand the process."

The doctor paused, and then went on: "There are very many examples of symbiosis and commensalism abounding on all suitable planets of the galaxy. So, too, are there examples of parasitism and—what virtually is worse—where the parasite kills the host, and these can be called parasitoids. We here, ladies and gentlemen, are not parasites, even less are we parasitoids. We are symbionts. We give to the copepod magna easy food, sanitary conditions and medical treatment, and we can dispose of unwanted parasites and predators."

He coughed and the screen died.

"I come now to the great universal and marvelous fact that followed consequent on Doctor Arliss's life work. I cannot stress too strongly that this is the keystone of the whole symbiosis idea. Telepathy has long been a dream of Homo sapiens. So far no experiments have succeeded. Man cannot speak mind to mind with man. But we know that man can speak mind to mind with alien beings. It seems as though whatever Deity created the universe provided us with this marvelous faculty so that man might not destroy all with whom he came into contact."

Wade's delight at the doctor's purple flourishes could not diminish his real concern and sympthy.

"When you receive your alice you will be able to contact his thoughts, in varying degrees of clarity, and I say to you all in the utmost sincerity that this is a priceless gift. Do not abuse it. When you symb—that is, when you enter into this partial telepathic communication—with your symbiont, you are partaking of one of the greatest wonders in the galaxy."

Men and women around Wade were buzzing with comment and excited talk. The doctor of symbiosis waited a moment for them to calm down. For those who had either not thought the problem through or had disregarded it, these facts of life in the galaxy came always with the shock of new ideas. For, really, why should telepathy exist between members of the same species when they were provided with other sensory means of communication? But, nature and evolution as always one jump ahead, when the mind of man met the mind of alien beings—truly alien—then the jump could be made unfettered by preconceived standards of routine communication.

For Matthew Wade, ex coord of Altimus, with those extra circuits in his brain switched off, the poignant taste of dead ashes—in his mind, not his mouth, his mind!—brought a moment of self-pity and self-disgust. What had he done when he'd walked out of C.I.D.G.?

His negation of his life had been necessary.

He had to believe that, else he might as well opt

out of the whole confusing, aching, duty-rupturing bedlam that was modern day life in the galaxy.

He fitted into the routine of life on Catspaw well enough to avoid too much comment. But his continual feeling of acting out a part in the company of ordinary human beings marked him out for eventual disaster. He felt forced to move on and move on among the stars. Once he had taken that first step from Altimus he had taken the first step on a road that had no end.

He tried to learn how to adapt to normalcy as he was still trying when he touched down on Ashramdrego. Life on Catspaw consisted of collecting monocerate, whooping it up in the mess on whichever one of the several bases over the planet you were stationed, and trying to live with your alice.

One day, out working the flats, a foursome consisting of the two brothers, Dav and Fered, himself and a girl from the copper planet of Chem-Sheffarre, her glistening skin tinged with a delicate green and her laughing couldn't-care-less attitude one to enchant at first and then to irritate, picked up a plaintive bleeping on their radios.

Investigating, they came across a collecting robot whose red-painted body and wildly waving tendrils had been trapped in a sharp-sided cleft in the rocks.

The copper planet girl laughed.

"He looks stupid!"

"Damn robots are stupid, always falling into situations they haven't the programming to get out of. A simple cleft in the rock—" Dav let out a gust of annoyance. Their copepod magnas slowed down and halted on the lip. Almost like riding a huge sixteen-limbed horse, symbiosis with a Catspaw copepod magna was; almost, for here an umbilical cord of life connected them in a symbiosis backed and enhanced by their quasi-telepathic links. They set about freeing the robot, who sqawked complainingly.

"Careful of my carapace! Mind my tendrils! I am Liang-Peng property and willful damage to any part of my structure will be followed by fines and wage deductions."

"Aw, wrap up, iron man," snarled Dav.

They hauled the robot out and sent him trundling off.

The girl from Chem-Sheffarre had designs on Fered, and Dav, not without a grunt of baffled lust, said: "Okay, you two. Go seek over the northeast quadrant. Wade and I will tackle the southwest. Meet up midday for grub."

As the copepods picked up speed, Dav shouted back: "And don't waste too much time on you-know-what, Fered! I want to fill our quota ahead of time and have a ball back at base. Lancelot here needs a head of steam, too."

Lancelot, Dav's alice, frolicked out a couple of pairs of legs, and Wade chuckled, letting Boris lope on.

"Guess Fered will make out all right," Dav chuckled. "And his alice has been eyeing the Chem-Sheffarre girl's alice, too, kinda sly."

You could get up to all kinds of erotic love-ins in the galaxy, without detracting from the essential whole healthiness of an orgy, when you were twinned with an alice.

"Fellow over in three squad was telling me his last stint they had giant wasps as alices." Dav must have symbed a reprimand to Lancelot for the cope-pod quietened down. "I said that'd sting me." Dav laughed. He must have thought it funny. "Beats me how they find 'em all."

"There's a natural propensity for organisms to huddle," Wade said, only half thinking of the conversation. "Even on Earth there were more parasites and symbionts than not. You take symbiotic cleaning—why fish keep a special place of ocean floor for cleaning up. Predators don't attack their normal victim fish there. They all troop along and wait in line to be cleaned up by the cleaner fish. The señoritas of Southern California were well known for cleaning up opal eyes and like that."

"Hey, prof, you ever been to Earth?"

How to answer?

Unable to answer, Wade said smoothly: "And it works in reverse, too. On Earth they have a big stock of alices waiting for alien visitors who can't breathe our air. Mostly it's the noble gases, inert on Earth but absolutely toxic to alien physiology; krypton, xenon, radon—that one nearly finished the Embassy from Tol'kedrida."

"Yeah, I heard about that. They tell me sloths are good alices. Didn't they try domestic cats, once?'"

Wade nodded. "A disaster. Pussy wouldn't play."

"Well, unless you can get something in return for your services, being an alice is not—"

"But of course!" Wade spoke up. "We people of Earth, and we're all Earthmen when it boils down, can't expect just to go off and *use* an alien animal for our own commercial profit. That's what Astir's tenets are all about. And an alice won't be a good symbiont if he's not benefiting by the arrangement, after all, his metabolism has to take over and do the work. We'd be those parasites the symbiotist was telling us about—"

"Or a parasitoid. They're poison."

No incongruity could be tenable here in men talking like this wearing or riding alices, for this was a vital part of their profession. On the symb-socket circuit your alice was your life.

Wade let Boris lead on to the dark brown and maroon pool ahead. The lake spread beneath overhanging jagged cliffs. The sky blazed its spectrum of unearthly color. Fumes coiled from the surface of the lake. The liquid was not water.

Here the copepods were at home. They plunged into the acid bath and Wade caught the clear pattern of pleasure. Boris splashed in, calling playfully to Lancelot.

Acid that would have seared the flesh from his bones and bubbled them into gray slime washed back like spring water in the pool below the spillway back home. . . . His blood, protecting his body by reason of his symbiotic relationship with his life support system, cleansed and adapted to life on this planet, pumped through his body and lungs and through the body and lung-trachea system of Boris.

"They'd need an armored hostile-environment suit here every day, let alone every week!" said Dav, following.

They dived below the surface.

"If that fool robot falls in here he'll dissolve so fine the best filter in the chem lab wouldn't strain him out!"

Truly, ruminated Wade, beginning the search for monocerate, the multifarious ways of human flesh pass all mortal limitations and leave mere steel and ceramics and plastics as the dead artifacts they are. . . .

That, he realized with a little start, was part of the Creed of Astir. Well, and wasn't it true?

Rough and ready Dav might be and, like the majority of his companions in the symb-socket circuits of the companies, irreverent and given to lewd oaths and flamboyant attitudes, at the core of the man his devout belief in the tenets of Astir hearted him—like them all.

"By Kildish!" rasped Dav, his voice hollowed and reechoed by the viscous liquids around him. "Lookit that!"

Growing magnificently in the ambient fluids the diamond mountain branched and rebranched, sparkling, oleaginous with running color, altogether glorious, rising like coral from the deep-sunken bed of the acid lake.

"Holy Mother of Astir! That's what I've been waiting to see all my life!"

Dav's voice slurred.

Wade's curiosity spurred him forward. Boris hung back. A clear though formed: "Danger!"

Sharp menacing shapes darted and flashed between the crystal caves and through the ogival openings.

"Shoulda been Fered here," Dav's grumbles broke and his symb thought broke into open speech: "Damn you, Lancelot! Get on! I wanta grab a handful, make sure I'm not dreaming!"

"Danger! Danger!"

"Take it easy, Dav. I'm sure Fered can join—"

"Too right, prof. Meaning you no harm, of course,

but Fered's my kid brother. This'll make ma's eyes pop!"

A roiling began in the acid. Colors streaked and broke. A breaking wave beneath the surface smashed about them, cavitating with atmosphere from the surface, roiling the lake into a maelstrom. Boris and Wade were flung helplessly like stones from a catapult, surgically joined, tumbling over and over through the murky acid.

When the turmoil quieted, Boris bore Wade back. Dav was sorely hurt.

Lancelot, too, barely lived.

"Danger, danger!" symbed Boris in panic.

How Wade got them out and back to the base he preferred not to recall. A long interval of painful effort, of unrelenting determination not to shirk this responsibility, a period of intense mental and physical agony, terminated in deft gentle hands, of a sprung bed, a hovermattress, and of terrestrial air blowing about his body.

"You only just made it, Wade," said the doctor, whose name might be Fanxter or Frankster. Whiteness all about him, cleanliness, sterility—and a bowl of miniroses on the windowsill.

"What happened?"

"Your comrade will live. But I'm afraid his alice is past recovery. Your own suffered in the ride. You ran into a Dentatus Rex. They are very rare, fortunately."

When they let Wade out of the hospital—he had to fight them to retain Lon Chaney, who had philosophically come through it all rolled into a sausage shape and cummerbunded around Wade's waist and up his spine—he found he had legal rights to opt out of the job and move on. He dithered.

Fered thanked him profusely, over and over again, for saving his brother.

"You did what few other men would've done, prof. Gee, a Dentatus Rex! They're awful!"

"Dav's a good sort, Fered. I had a—a responsibility to him. We've all got responsibilities to one another. That's the only way the galaxy can run."

How mocking the words! How trite the sentiments! And how searingly indicting of his own petty actions!

After Fered had seen Dav, he sidled up to Wade with the air of a conspirator at the New Year in Ancient Rome.

"Dav's told me about you-know-what. We'll be going there and carving ourselves a fortune. Dav wants you in, prof."

No decision need be taken now.

"That's nice of you, Fered. But I'm signing off this hitch. All legal. I'll be shipping out first spacer that makes planetfall."

He did, too. He shook the acids of Catspaw from his boots without a qualm that a normal man might understand. He wished Dav and Fered good luck with their moonlighting on the acid-drowned diamond mountain. The brothers had stumbled on the El Dorado dreamed of by all the symb-socketeers on the galactic symb-socket circuit. The provision of a small annulus venting into your neck gave you opportunities denied to those dependent on a space suit and clumsy air tanks strapped to their backs.

He'd enjoyed his brief flirtation on the circuit, finding excitement of a kind there. Finding a position with another big corporation had been easy with his qualifications and the recommendation of Liang-Peng. The Kriseman Corporation directed him straight to a berth handling computers in its personnel office readying for the mass invasion of symb-socketeers that would come with the harvest, filling in for a staff mysteriously depleted after some troubles or other. . . .

And so here he was on Ashramdrego, sitting on the edge of a pool of light in the symbiosis lab and talking to Doctor Marian Anstee.

He couldn't recall all that she had said, now. Not now. He could think, in all that welter, of only one statement—and he'd only been on planet seven days!

"You love, him, Marian? You love Doctor Overbeck? That's monstrous!"

X

SOME MEN CARRIED on an argument like a personal vendetta, a forefinger hooked over cigarette holder, jammed into a corner of the mouth and aimed at a shoulder. They jabbed. They scored points. They pleaded special cases and decried counter pleas. They hated opposition. They did not brook it.

"Why can't you argue to get at the answers, why can't you dissect problems instead of your opponent? Why don't you investigate problems in mutual instead of antagonistic terms?"

Doc Hedges in his impassioned way had not once employed a pair of dot-dots. The matter, then, surmised Wade, starting up from the bench where Marian Anstee stared at him, the tears collecting on her cheeks, must indeed be serious.

Into the laboratory stomped Doc Hedges, gesticulating, a huge plaster swathing his nose, rattling away at the keen, incisive form of Doctor Overbeck, whose butch haircut glistened like a host of the Crusades.

"I argue to make a point, doctor, not for fun."

"Oh, arguing for fun is one thing. Anything goes there. But this is different. Dee-dot-dot-em well different!"

Overbeck quite evidently found the whole scene beneath him. A man whose sole preoccupation was his chosen aim in life, he shared with that singleness of vision a dedication crippling when faced with phenomena that did not fit his own ideas. Overbeck said: "You're an ignorant lout."

"All I'm saying, doctor, all I've bee-dot-dot-dee had the chance of saying around here, is you should try another eff-dot-dot-gee tack! These confounded alices are bee-dot-dot-wye dangerous!"

Marian dabbed her eyes with a tissue. She sniffed.

"Him?" asked Wade again, careless of thus trampling on another person's feelings. "That?"

"You are just a frightened, senile, palsied husk, Doctor Hedges!" Overbeck's keen incisive voice had never cut more sharply. "You are a wreck, a disgrace to our profession. I have already spacegrammed a request for your recall and replacement by a younger man who—"

"You eff-dot-dot-gee cee-dot-dot-tee!" Hedges danced with baffled fury. "Can't you see anything plainly before your nose! You can't even talk like a proper doctor."

"Nor, I notice, do you. Cant medical talk is cheap.
I deal in deeper matters than mere morphological
terminology."

"These confounded alices are going to kill us all!"

"Rubbish!"

Marian's fingers caught and gripped around Wade's
wrist. She tugged. He saw her face, glimmering in
the light that pooled about the two wrangling
doctors and shed a penumbra of softening gentle-
ness about the bench against the wall. "Please, Mat—"

He hovered, hating not so much the scene as the
strange reactions to it he experienced as pure physical pain in his intestines. Psychosomatic love sickness, yet; and all in seven days!"

"Just because the squoodles happened to be handy,
and you picked them, all your confounded professional pride and blind bee-dot-dot-wye ignorance
and prejudice prevents you from changing your
mind. You're blinkered!"

Overbeck's face showed clearly his own high conception of his role in galactic society.

"The squoodles here happen to be just about the
most perfect form of alice ever discovered! Don't
you appreciate that? They are small enough to be
carried easily, they are delightful to look at, sensuous to stroke, and they have an astounding lung and
blood capacity. Why, they are the most perfect form
of life support system I've ever had the good fortune
to handle!"

"Just like a baby playing with a thermonuclear
fuse."

"Emotional claptrap, Doctor Hedges, is scarcely
polemic. If you've nothing else to offer—"

"Marian thinks they're dangerous!"

Wade heard Marian's gasp, a gasp of confusion, guilt and fear.

Overbeck stabbed with his cigarette holder.

"And the opinion of a young, inexperienced, highly emotional and nearly unstable young woman still fresh out of Symbiosis Academy weighs more with you than my own?"

"Yeah! Sure!"

"Because you have poisoned her mind against me—"

"No!" Marian whispered in agony. "Oh, no!"

Wade couldn't stand any more of this. He couldn't stand idly by and see Marian tortured.

He gently freed his wrist from her feverish clutch and moved forward, slowly but with a steady momentum that took him into the pool of light. He nodded to Overbeck and said: "Hey, Dot-Dot, your conk? All right, is it?"

"Wade?"

Overbeck's keen incisive gaze pierced him.

Wade cheerfully ignored the doctor of symbiosis, waited expectantly for the doctor of medicine to speak.

"Conk? Oh, you dod-dot idjit! That confounded spacer bloodied it up a bit. I'm all right." All the time he spoke with a muffled, somewhat wheezing sound that made Overbeck's accusation that he was a senile old wheezer seem all the more true.

"What are you doing in my laboratory, Wade?"

"Hearing about squoodles, for one thing."

"You were listening to our conversation?"

Hedges laughed nastily.

Wade nodded. "You took no pains to keep your keen, incisive voice down, Overbeck. I'd suggest you listen more carefully to what Doc Hedges has to say—"

Overbeck swelled. His cigarette holder described a snappish circle. "I'm telling you to clear out, Wade! Right now! You forget I hold authority—"

"You and Sternmire."

"Symbiotic treatment on planet is my concern, solely."

A voice, a soft, breathy, uncertain voice, picked that up from over Wade's shoulder.

"No, Doctor Overbeck. Not solely. Not since I came here at your request. Some of the responsibility is mine now."

"Marian!" exclaimed Dot-Dot. He peered. "That confounded spacer captain—"

"Doctor Anstee?" Overbeck slashed a glance between Wade and Marian. His thin lips tightened. "I see!"

"You don't see, Overbeck," said Wade with a truculence he found amazing. "And, come to think of it, that's your trouble. You don't see. Doctor Anstee was, well, she just needed my assistance to get down here to the lab for the experiment she has running and—"

He broke off as Marian's horrified gasp checked him, as Overbeck's brows came down.

"Experiment? Doctor Anstee, perhaps you had better explain."

Too late, Wade realized he should have realized. Reality had caught up tardily, as usual.

Marian spoke now in a voice that indicated he had completed the mental throws and had decided to opt for Wade's problematical answers and questions.

ON THE SYMB-SOCKET CIRCUIT

"I would have fully informed you of the whole experiment in the next few days, Doctor Overbeck. I am well aware of my own inexperience, of my youth, perhaps too much aware. But you, you are the greatest authority on symbiosis in the galaxy, now that Doctor Arliss is dead. Don't you think I had to consider very carefully—I had no sleep, I lost weight—it wasn't an, an easy, thing to do."

Hedges stumped forward and drew Marian Anstee to the lab seat. He pushed her down and stared back up at Overbeck defiantly.

"The girl's all in," he said. "As her doctor I can't let you go on."

Overbeck ignored him. "What experiment, Doctor Anstee?"

"I'm afraid the alices—"

"Yes, yes," Overbeck snapped impatiently. "We've been all through that before. What have you been up to?"

Hedges bristled and started to speak but Wade, with a little gesture, nodding his head, said suavely: "I think Marian is up to coping with this, Dot-Dot."

"Sheer sadism, sheer eff-dot-dot-sadism!"

"I'll explain this nontechnically, so Wade can understand." She glanced up, a swallow movement he found disturbing and appealing. "I feel, I have a suspicion, that he may be able, possibly can, help us. I don't know . . ."

Was his coord status beginning to show through?

"There are many different sorts of hem-pigments in nature, even on Earth we knew of hemoglobin, the one vertebrates use, and hemocyanin, which is blue, and hemerythrin, which is red like hemoglobin, and the very interesting one chlorocruorin, which

111

is green. There are others on other planets with parallel but variant evolution—"

"The girls from the copper planet, Chem-Sheffarre," put in Wade to indicate he followed.

"Yes. They're all respiratory pigments. Now hemoglobin, the one we use, consists of histone, globin, and an iron compound, heme with a porphyrin nucleus. They're all ready compounds of a protein group with a prosthetic group."

Talking, thinking herself back into her experiment, Marian Anstee stood up and walked across to her bench. The chimpanzees chirruped. The men followed.

Overbeck said, not quite sneering, not quite patronizing: "This is first year work, doctor. I admit I haven't studied your work in this part of the lab for some weeks, but if that is the sum, then—"

"Oh, no," she said, with a flash of spirit Wade found tremendously stimulating.

"Let the girl speak, if she has to," Doc Hedges rumbled. "Although my responsibility for my patient is making me—"

"I feel better and I took another pick-up pill." Marian smiled briefly at Doc Hedges. "You see, in all vertebrates the heme is practically the same, but there are marked differences in the globin between different species. And, a fact not widely advertised, hemoglobin isn't necessarily the most efficient form of oxygen reversing attachment pigment."

"You mean there could be people or animals with a more efficient bloodstream than our own?"

"In just this one item, yes. But the blood also does a great many more things than merely accept oxygen and discharge carbon dioxide. We can tolerate this ghastly atmosphere of Ashramdrego on our skins and in our lungs and our eyes—"

"You should have been down on Catspaw," said Wade. "Oh, sorry, go on, Marian."

"Yes, I am waiting, Doctor Anstee."

She swallowed and went on like a schooner tacking into a force seven wind.

"Now hemoglobin differs only as far as we can tell, or rather, the main difference is—I mean, it is very closely related to chlorophyll. In the molecule magnesium is substituted for iron. Now the cycle between plant life and animal life on planet is too well known for me to go over all that again. Suffice it to say that man needs plants to provide him with living materials evolution has denied him the means to obtain directly himself."

Wade relaxed perhaps fifteen percent from a total anxiety for the girl. She was talking now coherently and as though aware of her audience.

She led them to a shadowed corner and switched on an overhead light. A square outline showed, a cage covered by a black cloth. She fingered the draw cord, nervous still.

Doctor Overbeck uttered a snort. "You didn't seriously consider—" he said with a cutting contempt. "Not really, after all my work—?"

She lifted her head.

"I considered, Doctor Overbeck, that we were not symbiotic with the alices. My judgment is that we are parasitic upon them!"

Overbeck stepped back as though slapped across the face.

"That—" he stuttered. "That is a deadly insult, Doctor Anstee! I shall ask you to explain yourself.

You know the sacred duty of any doctor of symbiosis, the tenets of Astir! You know we cannot allow ourselves to parasitize any other living form!"

"I do know, and here on Ashramdrego we have that situation."

Driving across Overbeck's outrage, Wade said easily: "So you figured that as plants give oxygen, and we derive a lot from them, you'd—"

"Oh, I thought up a lot of impractical schemes. You could have a plant pot strapped to your back and grow a suitable large flowered plant, and curve the bell flower down over your head, to give you a constant supply of oxygen—in the right light!"

Hedges hooted.

Overbeck stood, face pale, lips compressed, condemning.

"But that way there'd be no protection from the unpleasant planetary phenomena, only a supply of oxygen. So I thought of introducing a vine form into the arteries and veins, so that a kind of tree would grow inside us."

"Delightful," sang Doc Hedges. "You have a loathsome imagination, beautiful though you are, Marian."

"Keep quiet, if that tomfoolery is all you can contribute!" said Overbeck. His eyes did not leave Marian.

"Oh, I'll keep dead quiet, dot-dot, quiet," sang Hedges again, capering around the laboratory.

"Ignore the buffoon." Overbeck was, Wade saw now, clearly and fascinatedly interested in Marian's developing argument. She reached out for the draw cord again, fingering it as though it were the rip cord of an antigrav life preserver.

"I collected various examples of plant life on Drego. I put in a lot of work. Had you been around this laboratory, Doctor Overbeck, you would have been proud of me."

"Get on with it!" Overbeck, prodded, at last burst out of his thin professional skin.

"I chose a heme suitable, and developed the cross-matching of the iron and the magnesium—"

"If you're going to say, Doctor Anstee, that you developed a blood that would function in a human being down here on Drego, then I beg to inform you that the notion of individuality tailoring human beings to various planetary conditions is a very ancient idea. It stemmed from the pregalactic freedom phase, when men didn't clearly see that movement in the galaxy would be so all encompassing. We want workers on Drego this month, and next month they must be on another planet where their specially Anstee-tailored blood would be useless. That's why the symb-socket circuits work."

His sarcasm did not move her.

"No, Doctor Overbeck, I didn't do that. I developed a plant capable of supporting life, I believe."

"Well, let us see!"

She drew the draw cord.

The drawn curtain revealed a cage, barred with inch thick steel, so that the poisonous atmosphere of Ashramdrego flowed freely in and out.

Then Marian Anstee gasped, looking away from the cage.

"Doctor Hedges!"

For Dot-Dot Hedges capered down the laboratory floor, dancing and singing, swinging in his arms the life-size skeleton of a Dregoan reptile, wired together, whose clicking bones castaneted a counterpoint to his own infantile song.

"That juvenile sickness, it's got Doc Hedges!"

But neither Overbeck nor Wade could look, neither could tear their eyes away from the cage and its occupant, who lay on the floor, struggling to breathe.

They saw a chimpanzee, feebly stretched out, obviously dying, its eyes glazed and its sides barely moving. As they stared, the light gleamed down on the chimpanzee's eyes, they winked once, and then the lids closed.

The chimpanzee was dead.

But even that could not distract their attention from the fur of the chimpanzee, from its face, hands, feet.

The dead chimpanzee was a brilliant emerald green.

XI

THE POISONOUS WINDS of Ashramdrego, whose baleful swathes circumscribed the planet in a fog of toxic hostility, blustered up into the beginnings of a gale as they left the CT Building. Doc Hedges had been tucked up safely inside breathing good terrestrial air. Now Wade, with one broad hand an implantation on Marian's waist and hip, guided her toward her room for the second time this night. Doctor Overbeck finished giving instructions to the medics about Doc Hedges.

"He died," Marian said, for the millionth time since

the green monkey's death. "And I killed him. Poor Samivel, he was one of my favorites."

"That's a centuries' old argument, Marian, and I don't propose to start it up here." Light and noise, laughter and the clink of bottles floated from the gym. "You're going back to bed. I know that pick-up pill won't last long!"

The poison wind soughed down the walks, bending flower heads, gleaming and scintillant in the lights of the complex. Colors writhed. The chiaroscuro effect would have blinded an Earthman without an Ashramdregoan born alice to sustain and a-dapt him.

"Doctor Overbeck is going to deduct not only the cost of the materials I used from my salary; but also —poor Samivel—he's going to charge me for him, too."

"That's damn ghoulish, Marian! Now, see here, you said you loved the creep, and—"

"He's not, Mat, he's not! He's absolutely dedicated. He's overworked under strain. Do you suppose he doesn't understand the magnitude of the problem here?"

"He has a pretty poor way of showing gratitude to you."

"To him, I'm just—just—"

"Now you go straight in to sleep. Take a bye-bye pill this time. If you're on to something promising with this peculiar hemoglobin-chlorophyll mix of yours then it'll be fully discussed in the morning." He added under his breath: "I'm going to see to that."

With Marian safely in her room, Wade, in walking with belligerent intent back to the gym, found it quite unnecessary to take a pick-up pill or to call on any artificial stimulant of medical science. He felt himself to be in perfect control, even with his extra circuits switched off, and he wanted very much to redress the wrong he considered had been done to Marian. By Astir! Here the poor girl was, caught in a hideous dilemma. She believes in Overbeck, regards him with the awe reserved for great surgeons and masters of symbiosis, and then she comes reluctantly to the conclusion that through his own pride and the prodding of the Kriseman Corporation in their greed for gerontidril, he could not reverse the decision he had made in haste and lacking essential data.

No wonder she hadn't acted like a normal human being.

Then Matthew Wade stopped stock still. How did he know how a normal human being behaved? He'd thought they were all alike, all a little subhuman, really, all like machine parts punched out by a cosmic chromosomic die.

Now he was being forced to accept that they were all different, all individuals. Marian was no machined part.

Somewhere, he saw now, his training had omitted to take into the equation the fact that if normal human beings were indeed all the same then one set of empirical attitudes would have taken care of his problems with them.

He thrust aside the confusion.

He headed purposefully toward the gym, whose light and noise splashed the telltale signs of an orgy onto the indifferent, blustery Dregoan night.

A shadow flitting toward him resolved into the

spidery, large-handed, flat-footed form of Baron
w'Prortal. A hiccup whether from the farmer or his
alice Wade neither knew nor cared, preceded him.
For a sudden tense moment Wade concentrated his
attention, and then relaxed; the chief farmer was
only approaching drunkenness, not the macabre juvenile sickness.

"G'night, hero—ero—ero!" chortled Baron w'Prortal,
gaily. Wade chuckled, then forged on toward the
gym. Wind blustered about him, stirring Sinbad's
fur, making Lon Chaney cling in tightly.

More shadows, this time urgent, decisive, closed
in.

Wade sighed.

Four of Kolok Trujillo's men, crewmen abroad his
starship, surrounded Wade. They wore uniforms.
Their alices humped and hiccuped uncomfortably.
Their faces, molded from the same source it seemed,
strained a blank and frightening vacuousness of vision upon him. They carried saps in their hands. They
smacked the saps against their open palms, joying in
the rich soggy sound.

"We've been waiting for you, Wade," one of them
said.

An irrevelant prod of delight at the absence of the
young lieutenant, Basil, who had cut in on his dance
with Cleo, surprised Wade. He hadn't known he'd
cared.

"This is the guy who beat up the skipper."

"Yeah! Well, we'll soon trim his ears for him.
Maybe jerk his alice some, make him jump a little—
huh?"

"Sure! Let's see him squirm!"

Wade had no relish, no training and, he suspected,

no real aptitude for a brawl. Takkarnia had been an exception. He looked for a way through the ring, a way to run.

Once he could break through them he could hunker down in a shadowed corner, and with Lon Chaney doing his stuff they'd never find him. He lifted on the balls of his feet.

The first sap whistled down. He blocked it with his left forearm and felt the shock of pain. He squirmed down, trying to bustle past, and the shock of the response pattern from Sinbad symbed into his mind like a scalpel.

Someone's fingers slithered off Sinbad's fur as the alice's single dagger tooth sliced down.

"Ow! The brute bit me!"

"Slug the creep!"

Blows showered on his body. Again he felt the pattern of anger and agony from Sinbad. He flailed out with his arms, his fists futilely bunched.

Before his face, as his own lashing fist fell short, he saw the down rushing sap. He tried to duck—and the sap halted in midair, was twisted up and back, and a stout fist shot from somewhere to connect cleanly on the chin of the spacer, who ooffled and collapsed untidily to the slabbed walk.

"You all right, Mat?"

The other spacers were running—no, another one was down, holding his belly and mewling like a castrated cat.

"I—I think so," he gasped. "Who?"

"Stinking punks space in all grand from the galaxy and think they own the symb-socket circuit!" Tom Martin's face swam before Wade's eyes. "They won't try that again."

"You let your other man get away, Tom," snapped Luis Perceau. He appeared holding the third galactic starship man's head under his arm, casually banging the man's nose every time he squirmed. "That accident out there in the geron plantation undermine your military strength or sump'n?"

Wade laughed.

"They were pulling Mat's alice," shouted Martin. The young D.D.O. looked enraged, the pallor gone from his face. "That's filthy!"

"Sure it is, but it happens. Give a guy a lever on another guy and he'll use it. That's human nature."

"Do you have a body attached to that head under your arm, Luis?" asked Wade a little headily himself.

"Huh? Oh, sure." Perceau smiled widely. He hit harder and then dropped the resultant unconscious body. "We spotted these no-goodniks slide out after the gallant captain crawled in. You musta done a good job on him, Mat."

Strange, how animal violence brought out the first name familiarity.

"He thought he was going to enjoy himself raping Marian Anstee—"

Tom Martin snapped up like a gyro hunting north. "The bastard! I'll fix him, so help me—"

"Hold it, boy!" Perceau's face remained unrelenting, his accents just as tough. "You know she's nuts over Doc Overbeck. You don't stand a chance."

Martin's shoulders slumped and he reached up to push his new alice back. "Sure. Sure, I know. But I —well, all the same, I'll fix his drive tubes!"

Had Wade made friends, here, with these two military men, the men he would have instinctively regarded as the least congenial company on the base?

He disliked Perceau, didn't he? And Tom Martin had become decidedly less interesting with his abrupt loss of interest in Plautus and Molière after the accident. Surely something was wrong? These men represented all that was bad about man in space, didn't they?

Just because they had saved him a beating—and there was Sinbad, too, and Lon Chaney—even that would be too simple a rebound. Yes, surely?

"You really all right, Mat?"

"Yes. Uh, thanks. Thanks for horning in. I was in for a bad time there. And my alice—"

"That's a filthy trick. I've seen it other planets."

They began to walk back to the gym, leaving the four unconscious gallants from the stars decorating the walk.

"They'll be too ashamed to make an issue of it," said Perceau with cocky certainty. "Blasted starship jockeys!"

Friction between humans, always friction. . . .

The orgy had simmered along nicely and was now erupting into a boil of lecherous activity. Wade noticed nothing exceptionally outré, searching the gym. Martin and Perceau, their duty done, dived in with a whoop. Wade circled the room.

He found Silas Sternmire disentangling himself from a pile of naked bodies, limbs and breasts, thighs and buttocks, straining and heaving in merry abandon, naturally. At this juncture in human societal growth copulation in dark corners and hotel bedrooms was for those permanently cognate in quasi-matrimony or intent on other goals. He wondered how Marian would have handled Captain

Kirkus, how she would have responded to himself, come to that.

As a symbiotist she might be expected not to have much sympathy for the personality that demanded darkness and seclusion before natural sex could take place.

That didn't include the girls from Chem-Sheffarre, of course. They remained a law unto their sweet selves.

He helped the director up and smoothed down his alice.

"It's just as well these alices don't demand love lives of their own!" puffed the director before he saw who had helped him.

Wade marveled. Old dough face making a funny?

With another sudden squirt up his giggle muscles he saw a white bejeweled arm reach unavailingly after Kolok Trujillo, who heaved himself out of the ruck. The corporation tycoon grunted and puffed his cheeks, slapped a rotating rump that happened to be passing and stood up, laughing.

Well, this seemed as good an occasion as any—

"About that game of marbles—"

"Oh, no!" yelped Trujillo, not yet fully back to being a tycoon of the galaxy. "I need a sit down and a drink. And then," he rubbed his stomach reflectively. "I saw a little thing in there I'm going to have to investigate, before this night is out."

The squirming, stumbling, laughing pile of naked bodies presented an almost irresistible invitation.

"Wade?" The director was visibly returning to being just that. "The marbles—I understand that you were not to blame. Mr. Perceau informed me of the situation. And there was your presence of mind with Tom Martin—"

"Sure," chimed in Trujillo. "He's the hero of the evening and we haven't seen him yet." He'd quite clearly decided to forget the earlier confrontation. "Let's get those drinks and a seat. I need a breather."

Sitting down at a table near the bar with a glass of some bland wine, Wade realized ruefully that this moment, after all, was not as propitious as he had expected. Sternmire and Trujillo wanted to talk big, as was their wont, and perforce Wade listened in.

He saw that they weren't even conscious that they were trying to impress him and that if challenged they would both have indignantly denied that any such display was necessary to men in their position. He'd seen blinkers like that on Altimus, only then the scale of the self-deception had been of so high an order that the sheer weight of terror it invoked had branded his decision onto his mind.

The Regnant, still wearing his yellow gown and swathed in his own aura of grim aloofness, drifted past. The two big men glanced after him, chatting, and because he set their minds working along time honored grooves, they began to talk about Altimus and the C.I.D.G.

"Those Regnants," said Sternmire. "They make my flesh creep."

"He's useful. And the Regnancy are a powerful body in the galaxy. They want their allocation of gerontidril with priority. You did a good deal with the bailiff from Altimus?"

At once both men adopted that half-scary, half-humorous mode of speech men had to take up when talking about a force in the galaxy only dimly understood and almost entirely misrepresented. For the power of Altimus was very real and very imminent and all encompassing.

Silas Sternmire's doughy features grimaced deprecatingly.

"I did a most satisfactory deal with the bailiff."

"Come off it, Silas! You and I both know you don't dicker with anyone from Altimus, not even a tipstaff. They tell you what is going to happen, and it happens. That's what they're in the galaxy for."

Sternmire drank huffily.

"So they run everything, or think they do. I've heard stories—"

Trujillo snorted. "Well, don't repeat them to me. I know which side my caviar's laid."

And this was the terrible tycoon, overlord of a million men!

Truly, considered Wade, silently listening, he had forgotten the dread power of Altimus.

"They say," Sternmire said after a pause, "that the galaxy has never been better run since the C.I.D.G. began. With all the many kingdoms and republics and confederations of planets all over, and the way scientific knowledge outruns all human limitations of control—"

"They had to have a coordinating body. It was lucky for us all that the mutant strain of the coords was isolated." Trujillo drank quickly. "I suppose I'm like everyone else. I often wondered what I would feel had I been chosen."

"They say you often know. . . ."

Wade hadn't even suspected. Not even when he went back to school for extra tests after the general tests everyone took. The bailiff in his blue cloak and his silver girdle talking to his mother and father, and their awed and stricken faces, had been his first intimation. . . .

"I wonder what it's like?" said Trujillo. "I mean, a member of a body like that. They're Parliament, Senate, Congress, Scientific Assembly, Monastery, psychiatrists to the galaxy!"

"They're more than poor bloody mortals, and that's for sure!"

"Or less," Wade put in so unexpectedly that both men swiveled in their seats to stare at him blankly.

At last Sternmire said stiffly: "If you're going to become tiresome again, Wade, I suggest you leave us."

"Sure. I need the goodwill of C.I.D.G. The coords of Altimus have *ways* of knowing what goes on in the galaxy."

Resentment, anger at abuse, contempt flowed over Wade.

"Of course," he said with prickly correctness. "Please forgive me. I was thinking of something else."

"That's the way to wind up—well, the coords don't even like anyone *talking* about it!"

Wade knew what he meant. Wade felt revulsion at what he meant.

The coords could examine the galaxy, as they must if they were to perform the function for which they existed, but he knew better than most how limited their powers were in reality. The terrible strength of myth was at work here, the mind-paralyzing power of myth.

What these two important men—leaving aside all jeering at their own connotations of their own importance—were discussing without talking about it was the cancer eating at the mind of the galaxy, at the painfully laborious construction of men. Law and justice, integrity and freedom, these were the things and ideals at stake in a galaxy that Matthew Wade had opted out of the coords of Altimus to join.

He knew with a clarity he could not doubt that Sternmire had searched diligently throughout his headquarters for a bug the bailiff might have left, knowing that the coords of Altimus needed no such clumsy method of mechanical and electronic contrivance to eavesdrop on his every word and action. Knowing that, believing that, feeling by that amount a debasement of his own status, Silas Sternmire would never find a spyeye or bug and that would merely convince him even more that the coords had his project under constant surveillance.

Poor, bumbling, normal human!

The coords had the galaxy scared witless.

Only this pressing problem down here on the surface of hostile Ashramdrego bulked more powerfully in the minds of the humans around him.

Even then, only some of the people here were cognizant of that problem.

For the others, well there was an orgy booming away, and the harvest was coming, and their own personal futures were set on the symb-socket circuits of the galaxy.

The subject of Altimus proving too explosive, Trujillo and Sternmire launched into other topics of mutual concern. Sternmire, as planetary director, rated a seat on the Kriseman Corporation's board well up toward the chairman's head-of-the-table seat. He and Trujillo could almost speak on equal terms, especially as Kriseman operated so much vaster a corporation than Kolok Trujillo's lone wolf outfit.

Wade learned that three more exceedingly influential corporation tycoons would be spacing in before the harvest. Those who could afford it wished to make personal deals with Sternmire for preferential supplies of gerontidril. For the first time, Wade wondered how Kriseman employees ranked. He had noticed an eagerness among the lower ranks—a relative term in a society served by robots and electroplasms—for service on Ashramdrego. Perhaps they had their perks, too. Good luck to 'em, he decided.

A localized war was being fought bitterly between two rival stellar groupings many hundreds of light-years away, and now the coords of Altimus were rousing themselves. The Regnancy had failed to stop the war. Recruits were openly being canvassed for on many worlds. The coords, it was said, would—and here followed a fantastic catalog of miracles that would be employed to bring the war to an end. About fifty percent of the wild imaginings were indeed open to use by Altimus. The Regnancy, those cold, yellow-clad aloof men who roamed the galaxy about their own business, had failed, and this rankled with them, an Order so proud, so dedicated, so absorbed in their own conceptions of where the galaxy should be going.

Whenever anyone spoke of the "galaxy" in these terms it was understood that what was referred to was the human-dominated portions of the galaxy, where terrestrial type planets were occupied by beings related to Homo sapiens, plus the few truly alien cultures so far integrated. Common sense, that great fertile attribute of the common man, indicated that it would be far too tiresome every time you wished to refer to the galaxy as it existed to repeat all that. That "galaxy" was a catchword for a myth, too. . . .

Colored lights flashed in psychedelic luxuriance across the ceiling and walls and the stomp and twang of the music seemed impossibly to grow louder and more insistent minute by minute.

The component parts of the orgy broke up and re-formed in fresh and more bizarre combinations.

Eva Vetri was there, her lithe brown body a fluid motion of grace. Alexander Lokoja was there, an ebon-skinned giant able to support a pyramidal mass of bodies. The fat little bejeweled man was there. Basil, the starship lieutenant was there. Wade saw no sign of Cleo. The yellow-robed Regnant prowled uncomfortably, unable to tear himself away unable to join in.

Olive Cameron walked in the door, looking relieved. She didn't spot Wade, taking an avoiding course around Trujillo and Sternmire. She threw off her nurse's uniform, donned when she'd been called to help with Dot-Dot Hedges, and she likewise threw herself onto the nearest heap of humanity, laughing and carefree now, grasping at hands and arms, burrowing in.

Wade felt a little happier about Hedges. The complex would need a doctor, a doctor of medicine, shortly.

Olive Cameron was followed by Doctor Overbeck. He looked at the orgy, spotted Sternmire and came straight on over, his face as keen and as incisive as ever, a parody of his own image.

Wade moved his chair nearer to the director. He was not above chicanery at this stage of the game.

"I don't suppose you've had a chance to read Doctor Anstee's preliminary reports on her new work, director," he said easily, with a deprecating smile at Trujilo, whose attention had been taken by Olive Cameron's full and luxurious figure. "I'm well aware how busy you are right now—"

"That's true, Wade, Astir knows!"

"Her work looks most promising. She's attempting to create new alice typecasts, using chlorophyll and hemoglobin matches. Unfortunately, Samivel, one of the test chimps died. But she's onto a most promising new line of inquiry. I don't like to mention our little contretemps. We never did get to finish that game of marbles, but your alice was—"

"I've washed the incident from my memory, Wade! I think it would be kinder of you not to refer to it again."

"Just so you know that Doctor Anstee is aware and is working to do something about it."

"Hmm. You think the alice caused it?"

"I wouldn't go so far as that, not yet. I'd be inclined to wait and see what Doctor Anstee turns up."

"Yes, she is, besides a most beautiful young lady, a most accomplished doctor of symbiosis."

"Someone talking about me?" broke in Overbeck, walking up briskly with a no-nonsense smile.

"Why, Doctor Overbeck! Sit down, have a drink." The director knew better than most the dependence of any symbiotic-organized planet and its director on the symbiotist in residence. He was carefully polite.

Overbeck sat, but he pushed the drink away.

"There's a little matter of departmental discipline I'd like to draw your attention to," he began.

Wade eased back, not smiling, waiting like a pike who has snaffled the bait and left the hook dangling bare.

Overbeck launched into a tirade about juniors taking on responsibility, the need for discipline. Wade sensed he was preparing the ground in general to a personal demand for a reprimand for Marian, and wished to mold the director to his views first.

The director cut him off. "Oh, by the way, doctor. I've been reading Doctor Anstee's reports on her new work and I consider it most valuable and rewarding. I think you have a most valuable assistant there. All credit to you for asking for her."

Wade did smile now. Overbeck tacked with the wind at once. "Oh—ah, yes. I'll talk to you about that when we have fuller data. The research is, ah, going reasonably well. I think I shall have to step in now. Doctor Anstee has reached the limit of her capacities."

Wade stood up. He looked down on Overbeck. "Think 'll turn in now. It's been a pleasant evening—if a little green in places."

Overbeck pierced him with a look.

Kolok Trujillo stood up, too, hoisting his stomach a millisecond after the rest of him.

"That girl who just dived in—you'll excuse me, folks? Oh, Wade, you've earned a spot of rest after your heroics with that stupid alice that took off. I'm taking out a hunting safari day after tomorrow." He looked down on Sternmire. "I'm sure the director will spare you for a week? Silas?"

"Oh, oh, yes, Kolok. Certainly. Wade, you take a

week off and go hunting with Mr. Trujillo. Your real work in Personnel will start with the beginning of harvest and that's probably a fortnight or so off now."

"Thank you, director, and thank you for asking me, Mr. Trujillo. I'll look forward to seeing some more of Ashramdrego."

XII

TOM MARTIN GLANCED up with a crooked smile as the fat bejeweled little man trotted past their tent on his way toward the cookhouse and chow. Ashram was sinking toward the horizon and the wild and so far untamed Nativate country rioted around them in grandiloquent washes of amethyst and topaz, of indigo and ocher.

"There goes Ergasilus." Martin's face showed his contempt.

Matthew Wade stood up and stretched. "I can stand chow right now, Tom. Safariing is a hungry pastime. Anyway, I know we agreed to call him Ergasilus; but it's always been argued that parasite wasn't quite the right meaning for Plautus's man in Captivi."

Martin joined him and they strolled through the dusk of the camp toward the cookhouse marquee. The expanded silvery marquee glowed with light, and the sound of men talking and laughing bounced against the alien air.

"Oh, I'm a little past—"

"I'd suggest a closer approximation would be Ben Jonson's Mosca, in Volpone. Now there was a parasite for you."

"Yeah. I'm not familiar with Volpone. Molière and—"

"Don't be frightened to stray outside the fold, Tom."

"Truth to tell, what with all the fuss back at HQ and my alice, and the Astir-forsaken ruptors, I'm beginning to have no time at all for research. Y'know, Mat," and here his voice took on a sharper tinge, "I wonder if it wouldn't be the best way, to dust 'em with a dose of hormone. Those ruptors are evil."

"They're just animals in an evolutionary ecology."

"Evil . . ."

They sat down to eat amidst the noise and bustle in a silent and contained bubble of apartness. All Wade's fears for Tom Martin seemed to be coming true. He felt sadness. Military minds were usually so closed.

They ate vac-packed cereding cooked in cider, with pineapples, all adapted to cultivation on Drego, with local juiceberries and a rich wine—not local vintage but an expensive item of Trujillo's starship larder. Wade kept popping the odd juiceberry into Sinbad's ever waiting feeding tube.

"See any eggs?"

Normally, eggs featured on every menu, for they were the favorite food of the alices, raw eggs, which the squoodles' single tooth could pierce, the tube suck dry, all in a matter of seconds.

A commotion began along the tables. The men of Trujillo's entourage made less fuss than the natives of Ashramdrego—any man or woman who lived here became in their eyes and the eyes of stellar visitors natives.

"Where's the goddamn eggs?"

"Hey, cooky! Bring on the eggs!"

It turned out that eggs had not been packed for the safari.

"No eggs, Sinbad," symbed Wade. "I'm sorry. You'll just have to subsist on whatever you fancy until we get back."

The response pattern fairly shivered into his mind, like icicles parting from a roof and driving onto his skull. Sinbad was not pleased. None of the alices was amused.

Alarm ghosted through Wade, the kind of alarm a coord could sense where a normal man would feel only annoyance.

That night the alices hiccuped a great deal, and the men and women laughed as they prepared for sleep. They'd flitted in a group of fliers over the Fractured Hills, away across the far line of cultivated plantations until they'd reached untamed Nativate country, and on the morrow they would set out to hunt ruptors and any other suitable game. They would be using rifles and various forms of hand weapons, as well as cameras, for ruptors were vermin.

Crawling into the double tent he shared with Martin, who had been sent along for two reasons: to give him a chance to recuperate from his experience, and since he wouldn't be up to his defense duties on the base, he could perform the necessary function of going along as the official Kriseman military authority with the safari, Wade halted. A vague shape floated past on the night wind.

He squinted his eyes up in the faint light and saw the bloated balloon of an orbovita drifting by, twirling gently from side to side, the tendrils hanging down quite limp and straight. Wade thought the eyes were boring directly into his own. The creature wafted on and vanished from sight beyond the larger central tent housing Trujillo.

Those lambent eyes haunted Wade. As with his experience in seeing ruptors alive for the first time, so now the living orbovita bulked so much larger and more splendidly than the dead specimen behind glass. The gas sac had bulged out for at least twenty feet, swollen and shining, proud and resplendent, somehow daunting and yet completely without menace.

Little fatty, Ergasilus, had been boasting that afternoon that he was going to put a crossbow bolt smack into an orbovita's gas sac. He wanted to see just how it would pop. Others had even been laying bets on the loudness of the explosion. Wade shook his head. The galaxy remained a savage and primeval quagmire despite the Regnancy, and despite, too, the coords of Altimus, whose avowed intention had nothing to do with morals.

Perhaps, if Altimus and the Regnancy had got together, as an old dream had suggested. . . . But they existed for disparate functions.

The Regnant had not come on the trip. Wade had borrowed a cine camera from Marian and promised to take care of it. He went to sleep thinking of her.

Whorls of dreams presented him with the macabre figure of Plautus's Pyrgopolynices, the Miles Gloriosus, the Boastful Soldier, armed in full exoskeletal space armor brandishing a full power Lee-Johns. When he peered through the quadruple face armor he saw the features of both Luis Perceau and Tom Martin inextricably entwined. The faces of Eva Vetri and Olive Cameron floated like twinned orbovitas, and Alexander Lokoja and Baron w'Prortal found their own features in the deadly intentness of diving ruptors. For the first time in a long while, he did not sleep well.

In the morning, checking their gear, Tom Martin grumbled: "These people of Trujillo's seem to think ruptors are some kind of joke."

"We know different, though, eh, Tom?"

Martin didn't rise to the bait.

"They'll learn," he said, with venomous grimness.

At Silas Sternmire's insistence the safari had come well supplied with lungs.

"Here we are walking about in an atmosphere that would kill us stone dead," Martin buckled the last magneclamp with a fierce snap. "I've always been the strongest supporter of the symb-socket circuit, and yet—and yet I'm glad we've a lung apiece along, Mat."

"It's quite a return to the bad old days of planetary exploration, when you had to carry all your air on your back, right?"

"If we had to rely on air tanks and archaic systems like that, we'd never have got geron cultivation going at all."

"Even with an oxygenator and an air converter running full blast at the camp, I think you're right."

They walked out to the central area where already the passage of boots had worn the ground clear. Dust puffed. The sun rose splendidly in sheets of green and blue and with gold and orange trickling down like smears of blood to the limned horizon. There was much clicking of guns and slapping of belts and aiming of cameras. Wade had experienced neither joy nor relief when informed that Captain Kirkus would not be accompanying the safari. One or two of the geron production people had come along on the invitation of Trujillo. Wade, like most of them, wore simple hunting gear, khaki or camouflage trousers and shirt, a floppy hat, and intended to hunt on foot. This ritualistic return to a hunting structure of the past, refusing modern scientific aids, represented a clear acceptance of the tenets of Astir, an understanding of the power of flesh and blood in an electronic and mechanistic universe.

For those people who intended to shoot their quarry, Wade felt pity. As a computer man in Personnel, of course, he had no power to forbid them.

At first he refused Martin's offer of a hand weapon.

"Come on, Mat. You never know. You remember last time?"

Martin slung his powerful, explosive projectile Wyalong-Green special. The rifle looked as tautly professional as its owner.

"Y'know, you might be right, Tom." Wade took the proffered gun, slipped it into his empty holster. Now how had he come to have buckled on a belt carrying a holster in the first place?

Martin strode ahead, saying: "When I went to military academy on Soldagda I never dreamed all that training would end up in being a D.D.O. shepherding a lot of silly people on a safari."

"You were trained on Dagda?"

"Sure. It was tough. I'd suggest most of my pals then are—oh, out doing all manner of exciting things in the galaxy."

"I never had any brothers or sisters; but when I

was a kid we often talked of getting a place on Dagda. It was a sort of dream with us, too."

"They train the best there. Their record of admirals and marshals and paladins is just about the best in the galaxy—hell, Mat—I'm maundering!"

"We kids didn't consider the chance of going to Dagda as maundering—" Wade halted. How to explain those far off days when he'd been a child? When he had had no clear-cut responsibilities? The arrival of the bailiff from Altimus had changed a very great deal more than a mere child's dreams.

With a few final words Tom Martin swung off to his flier in which he would flit over the safari policing everyone's actions. Terrans had been killed out hunting on wild planets before, and there was no guarantee that that habit would stop here on Ashramdrego.

Wade tapped his gun. Every day, it seemed to him, Martin sloughed off his old self and took on the attributes of Luis Perceau, and in that dubious progress the late coord of Altimus saw a dismaying reenactment of forces that had driven him into exile.

His own susceptibilities as a man had never been completely submerged in his status a a coord. He could feel the problem—unspoken, even generally unthought—of the people here on Drego as a personal pain. There must be something he could do about this latent yet smolderingly violent situation. Alerted, even a blind man could sense the undercurrents of disaster. The tragedy lay in that sheerly irreverent lack of knowledge and care.

Fear for Marian Anstee chilled him.

He tried to reassure himself with the obvious thought that the authorities knew what they were about. In a fortnight hordes of workers of he symb-socket circuit would space in for the harvest. Marian's alternative proposals might work out. What he himself wanted from life had not been any idea beyond a vague dissatisfaction and restlessness conjoined with his more concrete determination to opt out of the C.I.D.G. Now, any thoughts of permanency for the future had once more been destroyed.

He began to walk into the alien woods. Half an hour later, sweating and beginning to puff, he paused for a breather beneath the bent branches of a giant tree, whose leaves susurrated continuously and whose pendulous fruit hung down just out of reach, tantalizingly. The terrain was cut up into countless runnels and humps; roots of trees burst through the soil in serpentine loop; the thick detritus of a thousand years lay undisturbed about him.

Should a ruptor, or any other wild animal actually attack him, why then he might shoot in self-defense, but his ideas of humanity did not include wanton destruction for sport. He'd promised to bring back some startling cine shots for Marian, and this he would do if he could.

The purple-leaved bushes to his left, growing to head height, thrashed and a body moved through. He saw a head and neck like a drunken giraffe's, followed by a body the size and shape of a grand piano, supported on six legs a marathon runner would have envied. The animal's body fur was yellow and purple patched, soft and downy. It reached up and began peacefully to munch the hanging fruit.

Wade started filming, chuckling.

The silent mesh drive of the camera did not startle the animal, but when Wade, still chuckling, said gently: "Hey, pal, how's about sharing some of that fruit?" the animal, in a motion that began with its feet on the ground and ended with a fast-vanishing glimpse of a tufted tail some twenty feet in the air, took flight.

Wade sighed.

"I don't know what that fruit is, Sinbad, but it makes my mouth water."

Only a snappy, dry and irritable response pattern formed.

Sympathetically, Wade symbed: "Those eggs still bothering you?"

The response pattern sizzled.

"Tell you what, Sinbad, as soon as we get back to camp I'll arrange for a flier to bring an egg supply from HQ. I promise—if you're not happy without eggs then I'm not happy because you're not happy."

This time the response flared in Wade's mind with a sharpness and clarity he had never before experienced from Sinbad. Nothing like as coherent as the extended responses he had elicited from Boris, his copepod of Catspaw, yet this response contained the trembling hint of words, the promise of linguistic communication.

"All right, all right, Sinbad, you old glutton," Wade laughed, slinging the camera and moving on. "I'll see you right, never fear."

Men on the symb-socket circuit came to a planet and accepted the local alice and did their job enjoying themselves in the galaxy and joying in their work as its functional expression of leisure and then moved on. They could not hope to experience the deep and close bound ties that must inevitably spring up between a man and his alice over long periods. A man's alice was more than his best friend, a man's alice was his life.

"Now," said Wade, moving through the alien forest, "if only you had a love life, Sinbad. Some of the antics they got up to on Catspaw amazed even me. And I've heard stories of other planets and other alices that'd make your hair stand on end and dance a hornpipe—"

The repeater rip-crack explosions of an automatic rifle punctures the forest. A full clip of twenty-five sounds went off. Wade frowned. A hunter?

A woman screamed. Without stopping to think or to take any cognizance of the banality of the situation, Wade took off. He blundered through fronds and ferns and trailing lianas, tripping on the serpentine loops of tree roots, fending off sharp, scratching thorns. He had no real experience of life in the galaxy or of the sophistication of social relationships, but a woman in trouble on an alien planet had always been enough to arouse primitive feelings in a man and, supposing Homo sapiens still to have hair on its collectvie chest, always would.

Ducking under a down sweeping branch and straightening up, he glimpsed an orbovita glinting along through the branches, its sac glimmering with shadowed reflections from Ashram overhead. The floating wraith vanished beyond a fallen tree's tangle of parasitic growth. Wade ran on.

No more shots had followed and even to Wade firing a full clip empty meant panic.

Shafts of sunlight slanted down through the duskier boscage of the forest. A scent of alien saxifrage burst abruptly as he put a foot through a powder puff plant.

Looking for the clearing he knew he must find, Wade burst through a screen of pseudo-bamboos that screeched wind flutingly and lashed at him like maddened animate flails. His shirt ripped, with a response pattern of agony from Sinbad scorching his mind, he stumbled and fell into the clearing. Effortlessly, Lon Chaney, who had flicked away from the stinging lashes of the bamboo, circled himself over Wade and Sinbad and changed color to match the leaf-strewn forest floor.

The diving ruptor triggered past in a buzzing whirr of speed, his sting gouging a splinter of earth less than six inches from Wade's nose. Sweat dripped down that nose. Wade swallowed. Carefully, past Lon Chaney, he cocked an eye. The ruptor spiraled up, avoiding the tree branches with nonchalant ease, began to patrol.

"The dang thing knows we're down here somewhere," he said fretfully.

Sinbad's response pattern formed awful proportions.

Lon Chaney rippled as a tiny wind tumbled leaves.

The leaves piled up against a mound opposite Wade. He stared, and his mouth went dry.

In the clearing geron bushes grew wild, lining out in all directions, and half sprawled under the nearest the little, fat Ergasilus lay, his abdomen a single bloody wound.

The hand weapon Martin had passed across to Wade was a Kungsen energy weapon, a power gun of some destructive capacity. Wade used it with no conscious effort. Nacreous green fire washed over the ruptor and snuffed it into sludge.

Calmly, Wade stood up and looked down on the pathetic, crumpled, gutted little man.

The alice was gone.

Wade moved on and then, frantically hoping his eyes had played him a trick, that this moment of time might be reenacted and no longer contain what he saw, he shut his eyes and counted ten.

When he opened them again he still saw the naked form of Cleo, shining, lush and magnificent, dead on the floor of the forest. She was uninjured. She wore no alice.

A few paces on lay one of her admiring retinue, a young starship officer whose rigid hands still clutched his Smeeson rifle, and whose face expressed the thoughts of a man looking into hell. He no longer wore an alice.

A soughing sigh made Wade whirl.

An orbovita drifted past, his tendrils coiling and uncoiling like ropes thrown from a sinking ship. A ragged gash in his sac fluttered weakly, like the sails of that selfsame ship as they shuddered against the yards.

Wade lifted his Kungsen.

The orbovita drifted down and the tendrils caught at geron bushes, tethered the animal's upright posture. A quick movement of fingers at the ends of four or five tendrils began, curving up to the rip in the sac, transferring fluids from the mouth. Clearly, Wade could see, or thought he could see, a look of pain on that alien pug face.

A feeling of pity for the orbovita told Wade that it, too, had been ripped into by a ruptor's sting.

What had happened here took no great deductive powers to discover. What obsessed Wade was why what had happened had happened.

A simple safari party, out hunting, an orbovita and a ruptor. Wade couldn't continue to look at the lax white form of Cleo. How long before she would turn green, or whatever other horror Perceau had forecast would happen to a human who lost his alice, Wade didn't know. He turned away, saddened and disgusted, outraged by the waste.

He turned over a few geron bush leaves and as he had expected found many of the little yellow fuzzy ovoids.

All life formed chains.

These three dead humans had had no time to use their pocket radios before they'd died. Wade took out his own radio, which simple common sense indicated should always be carried by anyone out hunting on alien planets, and called up Martin in his flier.

"All dead?" Martin sounded horrified.

"And Cleo's stark naked. Don't hang about getting here, Tom."

"Check, Mat."

As he finished the brief conversation, Wade felt Sinbad utter a profane response pattern. The alice, he could guess, felt frightened and resentful. That beating from the animate bamboos hadn't helped, either.

"Take it easy, Sinbad."

The symbed response indicated disgust, fear, and —surely not?—indifference. The ravenous appetite for eggs formed a pattern that exploded in Wade's mind.

A petulance enshrined Sinbad's reactions now.

Wade shoved the Kungsen back in its holster. There was no further use for it at this juncture.

"I wish we could help that orbovita, Sinbad," he symbed. He felt concern over his alice's responses. Maybe he could jolly it away from those avaricious thoughts of eggs, rich and ripe and juicy, dripping golden. . . .

The response pattern formed sharp and snappish and preoccupied.

Only a whispering flutter heralded the second ruptor's piercing flight. It dove between tree branches and swept out into the clearing, its sting lowered and raked forward, aimed directly at the swollen but sagging orbovita's sac.

Again Matthew Wade did not have to think. He jerked the Kungsen out, lifted it, sprayed green fire in the path of the ruptor. The thing tried to reverse, but its speed carried it on and into dissolving destruction.

"Whew," said Wade, aloud. "We're having a busy morning." He shoved the gun away.

The orbovita had flung up a futile clump of tendrils before its face as the ruptor attacked. Its hold on the geron bushes broken, it drifted downwind on toward Wade. From the gap in its sac gas pulsed. Its eyes focused on Wade and again he felt that irrational sensation of awkward shame.

He saw movement in the bushes at his feet. A brown furred form appeared. A single sharp tooth struck into the egg held delicately between carmine claws. The tube began to suck.

The horror hit Wade long before Sinbad reacted. He felt that throbbing arterial connection between himself and his alice. He snatched out his radio, thumbed it open, screamed: "Tom! Hurry! Hurry!"

Sinbad moved on his shoulders.

Pain struck his neck. He thrust up a hand, letting the radio fall to the ground, tried to grab at Sinbad.

The alice eluded that desperately clutching hand.

Withdrawing his blood probe, the alice jumped swiftly from Wade's shoulder. He hit the ground, his claws clicking, began to burrow at the roots of the geron bushes.

Wade's mouth clamped shut. He pinched his own nose between forefinger and thumb. His eyes began to water.

Bereft of his life support system he stared about in paralytic horror on the poisonous vapors of this alien planet. Between him and death lay a lungful of air.

XIII

ON INHABITED PLANETS all over the human portions of this galaxy men and women went about their daily lives, performing the tasks nature and circumstance, habit and necessity imposed on them, helped in their endeavors by robots and electroplasms and by the cunning diversity of modern science and technology. On Takkat and Shurilala, on Pallas, on Chem-Sheffarre, on Sonpharaon and on the growing multitude of planets circling old Sol—on Mars and Ishtar and Ariadne and Elijah and Venus and, heartbreakingly combining all these widespread activities, on Earth herself—the efforts of facing the fresh tasks of the day consumed the energies of mankind.

Out of all those billions of people not one, not one single solitary individual, knew that down on poisonous Ashramdrego Matthew Wade faced death alone.

Jeweled and brilliant and cloaked mysteriously in dust clouds, pulsing with radiation and burning with squandered power, the galaxy turned ponderously in complete indifference. Liquid water? Oxygen-nitrogen air? Temperatures within a confiningly narrow band low down the scale of stellar fires? What did they mean? Pinkly squashy things with flesh and blood and bones? Who cared?

Curse geron bushes and cheating gerontidril! Blasphemies on ruptors! And, most of all, hate betraying treacherous filthy alices!

Here was where one symb-socketeer paid his personal price.

Oh, sure, Wade knew—theoretically, theoretically! —that a single gulp of Dregoan air would not kill him stone dead on the instant. His blood still was Dregoan blood. The stroma of his bone marrow and his terrestrial phagocytes, the fibrinogen, all the other complex structures of his circulatory system, were still as Sinbad had left them. But without his alice to maintain that Dregoan balance, his ancestral millennia of terrestrial evolutionary forces would begin to reassert themselves. An Earthman down here would breathe just once.

Already his lungs felt as though they enclosed a hydrogen bomb explosion.

His watering eyes stung.

He stared about, confused, jumbled, knowing he had no time to think long complicated thoughts.

Sinbad had deserted him to hunt eggs beneath the roots of the geron bushes.

Two more ruptors appeared at the far end of the clearing and at once, without hesitation, their wings blurred into a rainbow of speed. Their stings reached for him waspishly, twin exclamation points of destruction.

He lifted the Kungsen and then his arm faltered and the weapon drooped. Why bother? Why not the swift impalement of savage death in preference to the lingering deliquescence of toxic torture? The tenets of Astir had little to say to him now.

The orbovita swayed. Its tendrils writhed futilely as it tried to drag its clumsy body out of the way.

Surely, Wade's mind tried to think against the nonthought that obsessed him, surely it would be fitting to go out helping a sentient creature against animate blood lust?

He fired twice, awkwardly, and the diving ruptors dissolved in the wash of green fire.

He managed to think calmly of Marian Anstee.

He would not think of Altimus.

Marian's face and voice obsessed him. He could see her clearly, half smiling, shy, frightened, guilty over her clandestine experiments that now Doctor Overbeck would take and credit as his own. A green chimpanzee!

Matthew Wade thrust the Kungsen down into its holster. He straightened up. He held his lungs together like tattered rags over the chest of a scarecrow. He jumped for the orbovita. It stared at him without flinching. The torn edges of its sac fluttered. Wade grabbed those edges, pulling jaggedly down, using his feet on the animal's body to hoist himself up. He kicked wildly against geron leaves and orbo-vita tendrils. Then he thrust his head fully into the rip in the sac.

Clearly, he felt a tendril wrap around his thigh and lift him, hold him.

Like a man for the first time pulling the rip cord of a parachute, he opened his mouth and breathed.

He couldn't tell—not yet, not yet. The inside of the sac looked just like the inside of a red-veined, silvery balloon. Muscles reached up in thick bunches from the animal's body beneath. Wade climbed fur-ther, helped by the tendril, stood up on the orbo-vita's back within the sac. He breathed again.

The air within the sac smelled fresh and sweet, with a faint and pleasant scent of lavender. He got a better footing and breathed again.

He was still alive—and he felt fine.

Something twisted under his foot and he looked down. His mind recoiled in revulsion.

He bent and picked up the crossbow bolt.

So—Ergasilus and his boasting had resulted in this. The wound had not been caused by a ruptor, then, and by that much the estimation of humanity had been cheapened. At the rear of the gash torn by the crossbow bolt a thick vein pumped red blood. The blood dribbled down, stickily, to form a pool over the orbovita's back. Some of the blue red blood stained Wade's hunting trousers.

The orbovita would bleed to death unless the bleeding could be stopped, and the creature could not accomplish that for itself, situated as the wounded vein was within its own sac.

Feeling the preordained quality of his actions, fearful and yet in a manner at once full of renunciation and responsibility, Wade hunkered down. He wriggled his body about until he was lying with his neck alongside the ruptured vein when he could clasp it against his symb-socket. It might help him; it would save the orbovita.

"Well, old son," he was subvocalizing as he held the vein and the symb-socket. "This might hurt you more than it does me, to reverse the parental injunction, but it'll do until you can be patched up. I'll see to that."

The shock of the response pattern was overwhelmed in his astonishment at the quality of the reply.

Not words, not pure language, yet directed and controlled communication, channeled to correspond, the response pattern shared in its positiveness the conversational attitude he had experienced with Boris. The orbovita could communicate with him in a way far beyond the fuzzy emotional patterns of Sinbad.

Thanks, symbed the orbovita, thanks and gratitude; death of the ruptors, mindless killers; injuries mended and promise of permanent repair; oh yes, thanks, thanks and—welcome.

"It is I who should thank you and apologize for that filthy crossbow bolt," Wade symbed. "You don't seem surprised at—well, hardly talking, hardly telepathing—symbing with me."

"I have seen the children. I wondered at first—" Then the response pattern flowed away from concrete images and pseudo-words into its quick channeling of typical symbiosis, communications flow. Arrival of strange beings bringing stranger ways; midforms failing to eat; tearing up of ancient forests;

ruptors. . . . "Devilish ruptors!" Here once more the response pattern flowed over into concepts almost expressible in mere words.

That those thoughts were not, could not, be expressed in terrestrial words was clearly apparent in the word ruptor. What the orbovita called it summed up all the concepts of hell-fire and damnation—but the native Dregoan name wouldn't be ruptor. That had been changed from the original raptor, bird of prey, when the ruptors clearly were seen not to be birds.

As Wade waited the orbovita's thought responses flowed in and out, from formal response patterns to that more plastic conveyance of information a human could only represent to another person by words and those words ones understood by the auditor.

The orbovita was far from an insensate animal, Wade understood, and he found a growing respect for the macabre animal's quick and yet serene intelligence, and he thought appositely of those herbivorous teeth. Time began to drift by. Their conversation honed itself into an instrument capable of question and answer and innuendo and sly little giggle and a profounder understanding.

When enough time had passed for Wade to feel almost completely sure that both the air he breathed and the blood that passed between them were compatible—he could not be one hundred percent certain until a symbiotist had carried out laboratory checks—he saw the flier swoop in like a dragonfly over the surrounding trees. It circled twice and then landed near the bodies and Tom Martin alighted.

The orbovita stirred, its sac swelling now as the

air built up pressure against Wade's body stopper-
ing the gash.

Martin swung about and at once his Wyalong-
Green special slid into his hands. The muzzle lifted.

"Hold on, old son," symbed Wade. "This has got
to be done just right."

Patterns of anxiety, trust and confidence, awareness pulsed in his mind. A word formed, "Friend?"

"Yeah. I think so."

Wade took a deep breath and, perfectly aware that
if the blood from the orbovita was doing its job
he had nothing to fear, stuck his head out through
the gash and yelled: "Tcm!"

Martin looked as though he'd seen a djin stick
his head out of a whiskey bottle and pass the time
of day.

"What? Mat? Mat!"

Unstrung by relief, Wade laughed.

"I feel like Geronte in that notorious sack! Don't
act like Scapin—put that damned rifle down!"

"Your alice," shouted Martin. "Oh, oh, I see. I
don't have to keep asking what you went in that
galley for!"

With Martin's willing help and the aid of a first
aid kit they securely patched up the orbovita. Wade
wore a lung and felt the coldness of that impersonal
and imperfect artifact chill him as he let go of the
orbovita. Just before he severed his symbiotic com-
munion, he symbed: "Thanks, old son. I understand
a great deal more now than I did before we met.
And I promise, I'll do something about it. It all adds
up. In you I found the right question to most of the
answers. I shan't forget you."

Almost words, proto-words, formed the response

pattern. "Nor I, you." Help your people; the mid-forms, unable to resolve themselves; understand your problems; understand ours. The last pattern, clear and unambiguous: "Depil ruptors!"

They left the orbovita there as the flier climbed away. A party would return for the bodies. The safari, clearly, was over.

For Kolok Trujillo the shock of death came as a personal affront and an unwanted reminder that, despite gerontidril, he, too, like all humans, was mortal. Organ replacements and gerontidril and cybernetic marvels of medicine could not guarantee immortality, only stave off the sweeping scythe.

Matthew Wade flew back among the first refugees and immediately entered the Condition Terran Building where Marian Anstee fitted him with a new alice. The squoodle somehow seemed jejune to Wade with his new knowledge. He stroked the chestnut colored fur and symbed: "Hi, pal. You're Sinbad II —although why I should—well, never mind. Let's go get some eggs."

Sinbad II symbed a response pattern of immediate and absorbed hungry interest.

Wade thought very carefully who he would break what he had to say, considering the problem of Doctor Overbeck and Silas Sternmire, taking thought for the future.

As expected, Kolok Trujillo, after burying the three members of his party who had died: Cleo! Luscious, white-bodied, vibrant Cleo! Silly fat little Ergasilus and his profane crossbow, and the spaceman—spaced out without wasting a moment of time. He shed his alice in the CT Building before stalking out along the tunnel to the spaceport.

"Air, Silas," he said as a parting shot. "Domed cities filled with air and plenty of spare oxy cylinders. That's what you want."

"You've had a nasty shock, Kolok. But the ruptors killed your people. Symbiosis works. We know it does."

"Without symbiosis," added Overbeck incisively, "your gerontidril would cost a hundred times as much and you'd receive a thousandth part of what you have been allocated."

"I won't wait around for the harvest. Kriseman Corporation can spacemail it on to me."

"Good-bye, Kolok."

Trujillo went toward his starship without another word.

Soon after his ship had leaped from Ashramdrego the first of the ships bringing in the symb-socketeers for the harvest spaced in. Rough, tough, laughing men and women, with flashing eyes and teeth, brash, confident, decked out in finery from a hundred worlds, the travelers on the symb-socket circuit crowded into the C.T. Building. They accepted their alices with fine, casual professionalism. Queries about the alices' love lives were met with raucous shouts of disappointment and profane jokes at the absence of possible erotic combinations. Ashramdrego was new enough on the circuit. Wade buckled down to his job in Personnel, thankful still to be alive, undecided, abysmally unsure just what he should do.

Through his second escapade he was rapidly acquiring a legendary status, and this he hated. He could not forget the news-gathering capacity of the coords of Altimus. He looked among the newcomers for bailiffs and sighed with relief at their absence. The arrival of the harvesters made up his mind. He faced his responsibility. He acted.

XIV

THE HARVEST WOULD be early this season.

Matthew Wade's request for an immediate meeting with the director was met with a curt refusal, a reminder that if the tragedy had not brought him back to the base he would have been sent for, and a sharp admonition to attend to his crowding duties with the newly arrived Personnel.

Silas Sternmire, like everyone else, was fully committed to the harvest. Kriseman Corporation hadn't spent astronomical sums to send them down here just to have a good time.

Wade fumed. Trying to see the director, he was brusquely ordered back to work by Luis Perceau, whose major concern had now switched from ruptor control to piracy, bootlegging and theft control. Armed ships owned by the Kriseman Corporation patrolled in orbit around Ashramdrego. Disgusted with himself and yet aware that only by switching in those extra circuits in his brain would he really solve the problem without explanation, Wade went back to work. He'd give the danger spell a little breathing space yet, for there still remained a little time. . . . But only a little.

Almost everyone had gone out into the patterned fields, driven by Baron w'Prortal and his team, urged on by Hans Kremer who hovered like a nervous father over the imminence of his firstborn. In what few moments of rest he had, Wade took to sitting in the Split Infinitive trying to back up his decision to act with actual action.

Someone writing in a long gone culture had said that people went into bars to get drunk, an amazingly naïve and obviously untrue remark in a day of relatively understanding responsibility, but Wade began to have a vague glimmering of the hopelessness of life that alone could give rise to such inanity. He processed the arrivals and arranged everything necessary for their stay on Drego and apportioned the plantations according to need and supply of workers. Then he went into the fields himself.

"Right, Wade, you know the necessary," said Baron w'Prortal, his capable hands and spidery arms busy.

"One day they'll produce a cheap robot to do the job," said Wade, without humor. "Or an electroplasm."

Baron w'Prortal grimaced. "Kriseman Corporation isn't going to buy a lot of robots it can only use for about one week per season and keep them idle for the rest—apart from the fact that it takes a human to recognize when any individual geron head is ripe."

Wade grunted and started at the end of his row. All about him along the rows of this plantation men and women of the symb-socket circuit, laughing and chattering, skylarking, moved carefully from bush to bush, giving each geron head a tiny scratch with a thin, curved, razorlike tool. If the gashes remained dry they moved on. If the gashes oozed, however slightly, pungent purple milk viscidity, they cut the heads and slung them into their bags. Soon the atmosphere, despite or even because of their alices' breathing filters, became redolent with the heady, spicy, exciting smell of geron milk.

All week the workers would traverse the rows, checking the ripening heads each bush's separate flowers coming to full ripeness at different times. If a head was cut dry it was useless for gerontidril production and if allowed to ripen beyond that perfect viscidly oozing state would turn into a chemical poison equally useless. Each head had to be cut at exactly the right time and the leeway allowed was that of the time taken to travel from one end of a cultivated row to the other.

For Wade the exacting work bruised his sense of frustration. Mindless work, it was, fit only for the lowest mentalities. But then, the symb-socket workers had long ago discovered the work-leisure equations for themselves. The symb-socketeers, like most humans in the galaxy, had need only to work minimally—no, they did this for fun. The symb-socket circuit was for fun. Toward the close of the twentieth century, at that interface between the ancient dark world and the modern open galaxy, when men first began to question the propriety of work and the honesty of the "work dignifies" theories, a worker would have been wrapped and trapped in ideas of labor involving employer-labor relations, unions, rates of pay, hours of work—the work-leisure equations had arrived as a great healing salve to man's psyche.

Work did not ennoble, neither need it degrade. When those ancient "hippies" sought to break away from their culture they, usually incoherently for they were young, tried to grasp the problem honestly.

They quoted the even more ancient Greeks, equating slaves and automation on the strength of a few score automated industries among thousands. Ahead of their time, they remained a romantic figment of legend and sympathetic dead-ends, like anachronistic dodos, too early, not too late.

Then had come the work-leisure equations, which, when the circumvention of $e = m^2$ was opening up the galaxy had in like and parallel manner opened up man's social environment.

For: $L = N \div WxI$

Where L equals Leisure; N equals Need, W equals Work and I equals Invention.

The most profound turnover in human thinking, of course, had had to wait until the absolutely vital importance of L had been fully realized. Everything else stemmed from that L.

Wade, brushing sweat from his eyes, scratching geron heads, looking for the purple ooze and if it came cutting off the head, knew those work-leisure equations to be true. But his mind kept going round and round on orbovita, ruptor, squoodle and plomp, with the tantalizing picture of Marian Anstee dancing before his eyes like all the promised ecstasies of paradise.

In the evening as Ashram dropped in sheets of emerald and amethyst with the blood red trails brushing the horizon, the workers flew back to their various bases over the cultivated areas of this northern continent. Wade would make directly for the Split Infinitive. On the second night the place was wild with rumors.

"A whole dozen! All lying there, dead! I tell you, Mac, it's scary."

Alices, taking off, then. . . .

"This gerontidril they're going to distill from the geron heads; hell, Mac, why can't they stick to the old rejuvenation elixir? It's expensive and it's not as good as gerontidril, but it still works! Always has!"

"Kriseman Corporation is onto a good thing here on Ashramdrego. Gerontidril is the most wanted item in the galaxy!"

"Yeeah, well, Mac, I don't like those guys being found with their symb-sockets open and empty."

"Too right."

Slowly Matthew Wade put his untouched glass of wine down. Everywhere the symb-socketeers were discussing this unprecedented accident. Alices? Hell, man, they were a man's *life*.

"By Astir, Mac, someone ought to do something."

"You'll never get off planet. Kriseman's ships up there'll see to that—"

Wade felt all his commitments rising like bile.

His responsibilities had been shirked consistently, except in petty instances like running futilely after Brother Stanley and giving the kiss of life to Tom Martin and selfishly helping Marian Anstee. Why, after all, was he alive in the galaxy? What had he been born for? Given the human galaxy as it existed and starting from there, that for his life to mean anything at all, he must act for what he believed in.

Even if it killed him?

Altimus. . . .

Oh, Altimus, what they had done to him!

He found Marian Anstee in bed and roused her out, not too gently, and waited for her to dress, her face troubled and dark eyed and distressed.

"Mat? What?"

"We're going to see Sternmire. And Overbeck. Call the good doctor and tell him he'd better get over to the lab pronto." He managed to add, with a smile he shouldn't have attempted: "There's a good girl."

Frightened at his manner, she complied, and they made their way through the Dregoan night to the symbiosis lab.

Groups of symb-socketeers prowling the walks began to clump outside Star House. Yowls rose. Some of them were demanding to be let out of their contracts. They wanted to space out. Tom Martin and a squad of Kriseman military fronted Star House, nervously fingering weapons.

As Wade and Doctor Anstee hurried along, the violence simmered on the poisonous night air. They saw a cloud of ruptors diving in over the east end of the compound, flagrantly diving on symb-socketeers who shrieked and ran and sought sanctuary with those around Star House. Martin's men fired their weapons at the ruptors, who drew back sullenly. How long, wondered Wade sickly, how long before those weapons spouted on the humans?

Roused out by Doctor Overbeck's call, stimulated to anger by the tension and the fear on the night air, Silas Sternmire strode into the white lit lab.

"Now what's this all about, doctor? Luis is going to have to resort to extreme measures. I just don't understand what's got into these symb-sockeeers, I just don't."

"This is most irregular, Silas, but Doctor Anstee—"

"And what the hell are you doing here, Wade?"

Wade looked on them. Silas Sternmire, doughy face pulsing with puzzled anger. Silas Sternmire, incisive to the last, like a soldier standing to attention as the ship went down. Luis Perceau, grim and daunting, fingers clamped on his gun butt.

Wade said: "You're going to have to put everyone in the CT Building and call in air equipment. It's got to be done."

They roared at him.

He shouted them down, blazingly, viciously.

"Can't you trust the evidence of your own eyes? You know what's happening. The squoodles leave their symbionts."

"It happens sometimes, yes," snapped Sternmire. "But that's no reason—"

"It's every reason, surely," said Marian, frightened.

"The alices we're using here are the best there are," said Overbeck. His face showed clean-cut in the stark lighting, handsome, overpowering. "If this is all—"

"It's not all!" Wade breathed in, and fingered Sinbad II, and wondered when and if. . . . He told them again to listen but Sternmire rumbled through his words.

"You've been acting as though you were some paladin or other, Wade, ever since you've been here. You know we must cut the harvest within a week. The ripening doesn't begin before and ends sharply. I need every human worker I have. I just don't understand them."

Perceau, whose face expressed every military virtue, blasted an oath as the rippled sound of gunfire reached into the laboratory. "Those Astir-forsaken ruptors! I'll have to—" He stopped speaking, shocked into immobility by the sight of the Kungsen in Wade's hand.

161

"Oh, Mat!" Marian straightened beside him and put a hand on his other arm. "If this is the only way—"

"Now," said Matthew Wade. "You will listen for this language I believe you understand."

The distant sounds of shouting and gunshots and energy weapon discharges floated over the laboratory.

"The first thing you should know is that because of Doctor Overbeck's shut mind you did not obtain a full picture of your alices' life cycles."

"I know that!" Overbeck shouted livedly. "There wasn't time. There hasn't been time. Kriseman—"

"This juvenile sickness," went on Wade, jerking the gun to silence Overbeck. "It was the most natural thing to happen. Through the symbiosis between a man and his alice attitudes must cross-fertilize. And, you see, the squoodles are children."

"Children!"

"Well, it's obvious isn't it, when you think? Every time your alice gave you a squirt up the giggle muscles he was just being himself. Even you, Sternmire, absorbed some juvenility from your alice—"

"Marbles!"

"The plomps, oh, you knew all about them, didn't you? Hans Kremer told me. A symbiont on the geron leaves. You didn't trouble to find out where they came from—or where they went to, did you? Plomps turn into squoodles, plomps are babies, squoodles are children. There are intermediate pseudo-chrysalis stages."

Doctor Overbeck jerked his aquiline features forward like a vulture inspecting intestines.

"I'll accept that. The structures are similar. But, you said—where—what?"

"Orbovitas," said Wade.

Marian Anstee suddenly broke into a dazzling smile.

Perceau looked doubtfully at Overbeck.

Sternmire looked angry and ruffled and vicious.

"I managed to stay alive by breathing a pretty fair old air the orbovitas' store in their sacs to give them life, a helium-oxygen mix, I'd say. Their blood matched; naturally it would as it stays the same from their squoodle days. The plomps are symbionts on the leaves; then you, Overbeck, when they turn into squoodles, come along and make them into symbionts with men. They conform. That's why they were good. But they like eggs—"

"All the alices don't take off for eggs, Mat," said Marian softly. "That's not tenable, I'm afraid."

"No, but this is. The last lot of troubles occurred because it was time in their development for some of the squoodles to become sessile and a pseudo-chrysalis, eventually to break out as an orbovita. And that time has come again. That's why there's going to be a rash of alices taking off, so they can get ready to grow up!"

Sternmire came to life. "But not all of them! They must spend more than just one season as a squoodle. Therefore only a proportion will leave."

"And you'd take that chance!"

"With the Kriseman Corporation breathing down my neck, it's not a chance, it's a plain bare necessity."

Wade refused that and struggled on. "The eggs the squoodles like so much, the ones out beneath the roots of the geron bushes, are ruptor eggs.

There's been a noticeable increase in ruptors lately around the base—"

Overbeck sneered. "There hasn't been time for eggs the squoodles would have eaten but didn't to hatch out."

"Of course. The ruptors aren't stupid, either. They've noticed the lack of squoodles around here, saw they could lay their eggs safely. They've had a field day out in the plantations, eating the plomps—"

"What?"

"You heard. When they rip down a line of geron bushes they snip the leaf with their pincers well ahead of their body, then they jink in with their jaws to snatch the plomp off from beneath. I've watched ruptors at feeding time very carefully. It all forms a chain—"

"And the ruptors delight in puncturing the orbo-vitas' sacs," breathed Marian.

"What you're doing, Overbeck, is breeding out your alices and breeding up a race of ruptors."

Overbeck looked shattered. Sternmire swung his porcine face on his doctor of symbiosis.

"Could all this farrago be true, doctor?"

Overbeck gestured vaguely. "Yes—I suppose so."

"The irony is, Doctor Overbeck," said Wade primly, "that to be a good synthesist you need to be a good analyst."

Now the noise of gunfire and riot outside could no longer be ignored. Perceau, grandly ignoring Wade's gun in the process, took his own Kungsen out. His jaw looked like a plowshare.

"I know these symb-socketeers. A few brisk words and a smoothing gesture or two. They'll quiet."

"You can't ask them to carry on now, Sternmire!" pleaded Wade. He'd thought—but then, he still didn't really understand ordinary humans.

Sternmire huffed up. "Doctor Overbeck will re-assure them. They'll carry on according to contract. If there's any trouble then Luis will handle it. They're not armed; we are."

"But they don't have to work! They're down here for the fun, for the contrast to leisure, to see the galaxy! You'll kill a whole lot of them. I know—"

"You know a lot, Wade, and yet you know nothing. They've signed contracts with Kriseman. If that harvest isn't gathered in in the week, we're finished down here. It's not as if geron was like opium. At least you have to collect the milk from the poppies all in one single day. The symb-socketeers will stay on Drego until the harvest is in."

"But," said Wade, the sound of wave-lashed pebbles in his head. "But haven't you understood anything of what I've told you? The alices are due to metamorphose. Almost all of them. Within the week. You're going to have a planet full of dead symb-socketeers down here!"

Overbeck looked ill.

Perceau raced for the door holding his gun fore-arm high. He had his job to do.

"Marian! For God's sake—for the sake of Astir—tell this damn fool the score!"

Sternmire drew himself up. "Put away your gun, Wade. You can shoot me, but that will change nothing. I understand what you're saying and it makes no difference. There are some things you are efficient in. That harvest *must* be collected in, don't you see that? The galaxy is waiting for it. It's my job. We'll handle the alices somehow."

"You refuse, then?"

"Of course I refuse. What else did you expect?"

XV

WHEN THEY THRUST him into the compound's little plastic-metal walled jail, Tom Martin at the head of a squad of his military, looking more grimly professional than sorrowful, Wade insisted they leave him a lung. He no longer trusted Sinbad II.

He warned Marian, made her promise to keep a lung by her all the time. When Doc Hedges dropped by, the electroplasm left on guard by Perceau because no humans could be spared refused the G.P. entry. Hedges trailed off up the walk followed by a stream of profane dot-dots flying on the poisonous wind. He'd try to convince Sternmire, Wade guessed, and would be faced with that blank refusal to understand, that chilling obsession with the object for which they were all down here. It did make sense, Wade dimly perceived, but his own understanding of normal human beings had undergone a psychic trauma of disbelief.

When the symb-socketeers had been pacified by the judicious display of guns and the smooth talk of Perceau and the symbiotic reassurances of Overbeck, they went harvesting the next day with fliers patrolling stocked with lungs. Wade didn't have the feeling left to laugh hallowly.

Time was running out like air from a cracked spaceship.

Soon, as his orbovita hose had symbed to him, the squoodles would depart en masse, for this was the time of year, and this season more of the squoodles had been in captivity for the use of the humans than during the last time of the troubles. It all fitted. . . .

That evening Marion came in with a bottle of wine and a drawn, scared face that wrenched at Wade.

She stroked Sinbad II. She stroked his alice and said: "What are we going to do, Mat?"

"If no one can convince Sternmire—"

She poured wine nervously, spilling some. "If the coords of Altimus kept as strict observation on the symb-socket circuit as they do on other spheres of interest in the galaxy, on war and economic pressures and scientific inventions and mass migrations, then, perhaps—"

He shivered.

"They're terrible," he said, drinking feverishly.

"Mat!"

Somehow, he was talking, somehow, cradling her warm soft firmness in his arms, stroking her, seeking comfort from her breast, he was talking to her, telling her, speaking of the area in his life he had willed into negation and forgetfulness. Hardly coherently, yet willfully, now, now it was all coming out, speaking of secret forbidden things, letting it all pour out like a child.

"Oh, yes, Marian, oh, yes, I'm a coord. But I couldn't stand what they were doing to the concept of the C.I.D.G. That? That's the Coordinating Inter-Disciplinary Gestalt. It's easier to say what it isn't than to say what it is. Years ago they had the idea of synthesis, of interdisciplinary functions; yet Altimus is no mere information bank or computer ready to drag out bits of the entire sum of human knowledge and assemble them like cosmic jigsaws. Not that at all; and yet, something like that. I can communicate directly with a computer, you know."

She reacted. He held her tighter, not looking at her.

"You explained the concept of symbiosis and differing hemes to me in simple language. I'm speaking in simple language now. My mind has *powers* that enable me to reach into a computer and take part in its processes, to take what I need without necessity of going through clumsy language or cybernetic communications barriers. We on Altimus combine the sum of human knowledge and more, but we are still human beings, although my fellows forget that."

She swallowed convulsively. What was he doing to her?

"You—you're human, Mat."

"You love Overbeck. That's human. Despite all his faults, you love him. I'm at fault, Marian. I know my responsibility to the galaxy and to every little part of the galaxy, for the whole great grand show is made up of just those tiny parts."

He couldn't stop now. "We have as our function in life the idea of creating through our manipulation of knowledge a more perfect and more beautiful galaxy. Each tiny scrap of information gleaned all over the stars and planets can be examined by us and co-related to any other. But it is not mechanical, a computer is only a tool. Men must ordain, it is their fate. Wanted or not, it is their fate. And my fellow coords forget that. They seek to ordain to other men; instead of the servants of the galaxy they seek to become its masters. The syndrome is old and evil and corrupt, but it is still alive and vibrant in the galaxy."

She had found her voice. Like a mother, she said: "And you opted out. You couldn't stand to see the evil growing—"

"I ran away."

"And they are after you."

"They're after me. What they'll do to me if they catch me, I have ideas. But I won't think of them, no, I daren't!"

"Poor Mat! A coord of Altimus, and yet so much smaller than a simple human being—"

"Don't say that!"

She cradled him, flesh smooth against flesh, their alices touching.

"If we could send a message to Altimus," she said at last, "they would come here. They have that power, at least. They could order a halt to this insanity."

"They take little notice of the symb-socket circuit."

"But they would now. I'll have to get a message to them."

"But me, Marian! What about me?"

"I think you already know, Mat. It's what you were selected as a coord for, isn't it?"

He felt through his fear a marvel at her acceptance of him as a coord, one of those mythical beings of legendary Altimus. Probably the touch of their bodies, conjoined, their arms about each other, their tears wet on each other's cheeks, perhaps the deep feeling they recognized in each other, perhaps his desperate need of her, gave her a fuller understanding of her own power and pride.

"I believe a general call to Altimus will bring a bailiff?"

"Yes." He had to say it. She would bring a bailiff here to save Ashramdrego, and with him the lean wolfish tipstaffs—oh, Brother Stanley!

Gently she disengaged her naked limbs from his. Like a mother petting a child to sleep she touched him on the forehead, stroked his alice. She stood up and swiftly left the jail. The electroplasm, programmed, let her go.

Fifteen minutes later she was back, distraught.

"They won't let me into the radio shack! Oh, Mat, it's all over! We'll die, all of us, I feel it. The lungs won't last and the air manufacturing plant in the CT Building is entirely incapable of supplying the wants of all the symb-socketeers."

"We've failed then."

Softly, she said: "At least, you won't have to go back and face the coords of Altimus."

He couldn't answer.

Those extra circuits in his brain seemed to be etching fiery lines of condemnation into his very being.

"A dead planet," she said. And again, crooning the words: "A world of poison gas where every human being is dead."

"No, no, Marian, no! You can symbiote with the orbovitas! They're fine people! They proved they are intelligent by their concern over their young. Driven away by the menace of the ruptors, they still tried to get back." He sought to draw the tattered shreds of his honor about him. "That is what will happen. You must work on it. Your own plant experiments must take this course, for, Marian, even though I— even though I—" he couldn't phrase that. He said flatly: "You were wrong, too, just as was Overbeck. The orbovitas can give us a perfect match, and in symbiosis we can give them defense against the ruptors and a controlled geron growth. Don't you see?"

She smiled and nestled down again.

"Doctor Overbeck has faded, Mat. What you say is true, all of it. But men will enter into symbiotic partnership with the orbovitas in the future. All of us down here will be long dead by then."

"Some will survive, they must."

"Perhaps. It doesn't matter. My own alice is showing positive signs of uneasiness, friskiness. She'll take off very soon. . . ."

He didn't want to believe that. Surely, of them all, the doctor of symbiosis herself would not suffer, could not, surely not, never, no. . . . No?

He started back. Over her smooth naked shoulder the alice stirred, hiccuping, carmine claws stretching and flexing.

"No, Marian, I didn't believe—no—look, you must get into the CT Building at once. At once. They need you to help them. You must go to the CT Building now and tell them about the orbovitas. Once you've rid the place of the ruptors, the orbovitas will come back. The squoodles will turn into orbovitas, you'll be all right." He didn't know what he was saying, holding her slenderness in his arms, shaking her, conscious of her warmth and scent and closeness. . . .

"It's no good, Mat." Her arms twined about him again, quieting him, soothing him even as they aroused in him other pungent emotions. "You wouldn't believe about the director, would you? And Luis, blindly devoted to his duty and the commands of his superiors. And Doctor Overbeck—" Her voice faltered, then she went on strongly: "I did love him, Mat. I did. But even love can be killed by stupidity and single-minded obsession. He can never see why I loved him, nor why I do not love him any longer."

"I—Marian—"

She shushed him. The warmth of her body encompassed him. Her golden hair stroked him. "I know, Mat. I've known from the minute you knew.

He thought of many things in that moment, chaotic, fragmentary, precious, ridiculous things. This girl, an ordinary human, and he, a coord of Altimus. How the galaxy feared Altimus. And how Altimus had distorted that original pure concept of interdisciplinary service. He stroked her alice. His early concern at the lack of symb communication was fully explained by the alice's immaturity, and that very childishness, too, explained their lack of personality. A man and his alice, twinned beings in love and service, must inevitably grow together as a single entity. Men had stayed down on inhospitable planets and refused to rejoin the symb-socket circuit for love of their alices. He could understand that now.

He looked across the cell where the two lungs had been piled. Forty-five minutes, an hour of air, and then. . . .

The idea of breaking out and finding two orbovitas and symbing with them crossed his mind to be rejected as a feverish dream. Electroplasms, military men with guns, acting on the paranoiac orders from the director would stop them—dead.

"Listen, Marian," he whispered unsteadily. "You can pass freely outside. If you won't go to the CT Building, then you must go out into the fields and find an orbovita. They are friendly. They understand about their children and us. You must enter into symbiosis with an orbovita. They are not repulsive animals, far from it." He spoke rapidly and with a brilliance of coherence that astounded him. He felt as though he was wandering. "You must join up with an orbovita. When the others are all dead you will be alive. You will be safe. The ships will come in to take away the gerontidril they'll believe Alexander Lokoja has distilled, and—"

She nestled closer. "I shall stay with you, Mat."

"But—"

"I want you, Mat, now, before we die."

Her alice rippled. Its carmine claws slipped across her bare silky skin. She put up a hand automatically to stroke the shining pelt. She felt the change and her face crumpled.

He saw and he thought: *"Better to die than face the coords of Altimus! Far better I die than that!"*

He could switch in those extra circuits in his brain, enter into that rarefied state existing between the coords they could call only a gestalt, wherein each coord could connect directly with every other coord and thus bring to bear on any problem the force and impact, the power and precision of a single mind. He could switch himself back on, and at once become more than human and less than human. He could rejoin that mystical union wherein each individual remained true to himself and yet partook at the table of superhuman capacities. Oh, yes, he could do that. He could call on the coords of Altimus for help. They would send their bailiff and their tip-staffs, and they would have these willful, blind and foolish people of Ashramdrego from the obsession of duty and greed and fear. And they would come for Matthew Wade and take him back to Altimus.

He could.

He could. . . .

He would sooner die right now, but he could call on Altimus. . . .

Marian's alice slipped from her neck, her shoulders, her breasts, sliding down over the smooth silky skin, warm and soft and sweet smelling. It jumped with obscene agility to the floor. It dived through the bars of the jail. The lung in Wade's hands felt cold and ugly.

Marian shook her head wildly, her mouth closed. She reached for Wade, clamped her mouth on his. He surrendered himself to the kiss, to the kiss of life —and the kiss of death.

Distorted fragments of his past life paraded past his whirling mind with a terminal jollity that heralded the end of the procession. He could. . . . He dared not because he was too frightened. But this woman, this slip of a girl all naked in his arms, joined in a life-giving kiss. He dared not? *He dared not?*

How could a coord of Altimus not dare anything at all in this galaxy?

Joyfully, Matthew Wade switched on those extra circuits in his mind and called out for the arbiters of life and death.